She stared at him, confused. "Why would I need a nanny?

"I haven't even been chosen for adoption yet."

"I was talking about now, for the boys," Jeb interjected amiably.

Cady blinked in surprise. "Just because *you* couldn't last a week…"

Jeb braced his hands on his waist. "How long I could hang in here is hardly the point. Although, for the record, I could easily weather two weeks."

Which, coincidentally, was exactly the amount of time she was staying in Laramie.

Cady scoffed and slid right back off the stool. She angled her chin at him. "Want to bet?"

"Yes." Jeb studied her just as contentiously. "As a matter of fact, Cady," he drawled, grinning, "I do."

Dear Reader,

Starting a family is a huge responsibility. It is a twenty-four-hour-a-day, seven-day-a-week, fifty-two-weeks-a-year commitment that lasts the rest of your lives.

Cady Keilor is ready for it. Nearly thirty-four, she has given up on having her babies the old-fashioned way—by marrying the man she loves—and is ready to adopt as a single mom.

Jeb McCabe is not ready to commit to anything beyond his lifelong friendship with Cady.

He is, however, ready to lend a hand whenever his good friend needs him. And, as she takes on the babysitting challenge of her lifetime to gain more parenting experience, and prepares to finally get the family of her own that she has always wanted, she *really* needs him.

Cady doesn't *want* to need Jeb any more than Jeb *wants* to make plans that extend beyond the happiness of the present. Unfortunately, she is struggling. So Cady looks to the one man—the only man—who springs to mind to help her out. Jeb McCabe. One of the legendary Texas McCabes, Jeb has the ability to "form a successful, happy family" in his genes. For Jeb, parenting is as easy as breathing. Which makes Cady wonder…is loving that easy for Jeb, too?

Happy reading!

Cathy Gillen Thacker

Her Cowboy Daddy

CATHY GILLEN THACKER

TORONTO NEW YORK LONDON
AMSTERDAM PARIS SYDNEY HAMBURG
STOCKHOLM ATHENS TOKYO MILAN MADRID
PRAGUE WARSAW BUDAPEST AUCKLAND

Recycling programs
for this product may
not exist in your area.

ISBN-13: 978-0-373-75367-3

HER COWBOY DADDY

ABOUT THE AUTHOR

Cathy Gillen Thacker is married and a mother of three. She and her husband spent eighteen years in Texas and now reside in North Carolina. Her mysteries, romantic comedies and heartwarming family stories have made numerous appearances on bestseller lists, but her best reward, she says, is knowing one of her books made someone's day a little brighter. A popular Harlequin Books author for many years, she loves telling passionate stories with happy endings, and thinks nothing beats a good romance and a hot cup of tea! You can visit Cathy's website at www.cathygillenthacker.com for more information on her upcoming and previously published books, recipes and a list of her favorite things.

Books by Cathy Gillen Thacker

HARLEQUIN AMERICAN ROMANCE

Chapter One

The young assistant's jaw dropped when Jeb McCabe paused in the doorway of the elegantly appointed office. She turned to the stunning boss-lady Jeb had come to see. "Wow, Cady, you weren't kidding when you said you knew just the right guy to hire! That, is one sexy cowboy."

Grinning, Jeb strolled into Cady Keilor's office on the executive floor, of the Texas Star Marketing Group. "Did you pay her to say that?"

Cady tossed him a wry look before giving him a warm and welcoming hug. "No, I did not. And for good reason. Your considerable male ego does not need any further boosting."

"Hey—" Jeb spread his hands wide "—can I help it if I'm just naturally drop-dead handsome?"

Cady rolled her eyes. Making it clear that she had never found him in the least bit sexually attractive. Which was why, Jeb thought, they were such good pals, and had been since they were in high school. Because, given the lack of chemistry on her part, nothing else was ever going to be possible.

"So I...made a mistake then?" The tenderfoot next to Cady cringed in embarrassment.

The twenty-something kid reminded Jeb of Cady in her pre-executive days, when she'd constantly been in the shadow of her glamorous and accomplished older sister, Suki. The days before Cady had come into her own, too.

"Jeb isn't the spokesperson for the Hanover Horseshoes," Cady explained kindly. "I haven't selected anyone yet for the campaign."

"Oh. Dear." The young woman blushed to the roots of her carrot-red hair.

"It's okay," Jeb quipped with exaggerated seriousness. "I'm often mistaken for a male model."

"Actually," Cady murmured, turning her gaze back to Jeb, "in your rodeo days, you graced more than one fancy poster, McCabe."

But his rodeo days—and the "heartbreaker" phase that had deliberately followed—were long over.

Not about to go down memory lane, he turned to the awkward apprentice. "And you're...?"

She clutched her notepad and pen to her chest. "Marissa Adams, Cady's new administrative assistant."

Jeb tipped the brim of his hat at her. "Pleased to meet you, Marissa. I'm Jeb."

"Nice to meet you, too," she murmured shyly.

Cady gathered up the reports on her desk and put them in a folder. Conversationally, she continued, "Jeb is an old and very dear friend from my hometown of Laramie."

Jeb gave her an exaggerated once-over. That they had an audience made the mutual ribbing all the more fun. "Watch who you're calling old, sweetheart." He sent Cady a teasing look. "You're the one with the birthday coming up."

She winced at the mere mention of the upcoming celebration.

Jeb realized the age thing remained a sore subject. Although he didn't see why, since he and Cady had been born in the same calendar year and *he* was happy. Maybe it was because they both wanted such different things out of life?

Determined to lift the sudden downshift in the mood, he informed the still confused Marissa, "I had my birthday a couple of months ago. I'm thirty-four."

Cady made a face at Jeb, resenting his easy acceptance of his age.

Which prompted him to add, even more devilishly, "And available." He winked playfully at both women. "In case anyone is asking."

Shocked, Marissa laughed out loud.

"Jeb's kidding," Cady corrected sternly, as if a great faux pas had been made. "He's not available."

Actually, he was.

He mocked Cady with an indignant look.

Cady lifted a staying hand. "There's no question Jeb is a nice and very charming guy, Marissa. He's from a great family and he makes a terrific pal, but…beyond that…"

Jeb was off-limits.

And not just to Cady's assistant.

Legend had it, to any woman with any sense.

Marissa still looked confused, so Jeb added the facts. "What Cady won't tell you is that I got cold feet and left my fiancée at the altar ten years ago. I haven't been serious about a woman since. Bottom line," he confessed matter-of-factly, "I'm a very bad bet. So, you and every other woman in this workplace would be wise to stay away from me."

Marissa sighed. "That's too bad," she said wistfully, not all that discouraged. "Because you really are cute—for an old guy."

This time, Cady laughed. Then, getting back to business, she handed the folder to Marissa.

Still smiling shyly, her assistant swept out shutting the door behind her.

Once Cady and Jeb were alone, he couldn't help but confront her about her comments. "Must you always warn women away?" he demanded. If he didn't know better, he'd think she was jealous. Or, as she had claimed on more than one occasion, just way too picky on *his* behalf.

Cady shrugged, not the least apologetic, and replied frankly, "She's too young for you. And way too naïve. You'd break her heart in no time flat and you wouldn't mean to."

"Or she'd break mine," he ventured.

Abruptly, Cady looked as distressed about the possibility as he felt. Then she smiled, obviously knowing, as did Jeb, that that just wasn't possible. He'd have to be interested first…. And unbeknownst to Cady, the only women who really intrigued him were stunning Texas go-getters like the gal in front of him.

He moved closer to the floor-to-ceiling windows and turned his eyes away from her all-knowing gaze, to the spectacular view of downtown Houston. Another beat of silence fell. Their arsenal of repartee momentarily exhausted, the only thing left was an overabundance of feeling he was determined not to give in to.

"So what is this news you had to tell me in person?"

he asked finally, noting the way Cady's stylish dress clung to her figure.

Maybe it was because she was so much smaller and more delicately built compared to his own tall, rangy frame, but he always felt the need to protect her.

She flushed and finally lowered the barbed wire fence she kept around her heart. "I'm sorry I was so mysterious on the phone."

Jeb took in the riot of pink color staining her pretty face, the uncertain twist of her soft, voluptuous lips. He wondered if she knew how pretty she looked, standing there in the late afternoon sunlight. Or how much he wished he could go after her, with any chance of success.

He shrugged, letting her know her demand was no big deal. "I was in the vicinity anyway, delivering livestock for a county rodeo." Working to keep his feelings in check, he nudged her arm playfully. "And you're still stalling. My question is…why?" Usually, Cady cut straight to the chase.

She tensed and turned toward him, resting a buff bare shoulder against the wall of tinted glass.

In deference to the intense summer heat, she wore a sexy-as-all-get-out hot pink sheath and matching heels. She ran a hand through her hair, pushing the thick, golden-brown mane away from her face. Her whiskey-colored eyes turning serious, she gazed up at him. "You remember the adoption service I signed up with four years ago?"

The one that had put her through a ton of home studies and evaluations, with very little result? Jeb studied the complex emotions in her wide-set eyes. "The Stork Agency," he recollected easily.

Cady's chin trembled with excitement. "Well, it's finally happened. They think they might have a baby for me. I still have to meet the pregnant teenager. Because it's an open adoption, and we'll be in contact with one another as the child grows up, we're going to need to feel compatible with each other, to proceed. But there's a chance I'm going to get the baby I want so very much."

"And you're nervous," Jeb guessed.

Cady knotted her hands in front of her. She drew a long, quavering breath. "Very."

Silence fell as they contemplated how much was suddenly on the line.

"What if she doesn't like me?" she asked finally.

Jeb bolstered Cady's flagging spirits with a reassuring look. "That's impossible."

"What if she doesn't think I'm mother material?"

Jeb had never met a more loving, caring woman. "We know you are."

Cady swallowed, still on edge.

He covered her hand with his own and gave her a searching look. "What is it you want to ask me?"

Cady relaxed and lifted her face up to his. "Will you come with me?"

There were a million reasons why Jeb should say no. And a very compelling one why he should say yes. They were friends and she needed him. He wasn't going to let her down.

He drew her close for a warm, companionable hug. "Of course I will," he murmured.

CADY INSTANTLY FELT BETTER the moment Jeb said yes, and even more comforted when he wrapped her in a friendly bear hug that spoke volumes about his casual affection for her.

The truth was, she always felt good when she was with Greta and Shane McCabe's oldest son. Calmer, more content somehow. As if no matter what happened, everything would turn out all right.

Part of it was the fact she and Jeb were both native Texans and had never lost the inherent practicality and friendliness that came from being reared in a small West Texas town.

Laramie was a place where kindness was de rigueur and neighbors looked out for each other. Self-made men and women abounded, and families like her own—of more modest beginnings—were treated with the same respect as prominent families like the McCabes, Carrigans, and Lockharts.

Ambition combined with hard work was a commodity everyone shared. Hence, the possibilities for everyone's future seemed limitless, because one never knew when a big idea or a bold business plan, or even a personal quest—like the one she had now—would come to fruition.

When they were kids, Jeb had been part of the popular crowd. As had Cady's older sister, Suki.

Cady had been a wallflower. Yet Jeb had never treated her as such. Instead, he'd made sure she was always included and made to feel as special as everyone else.

Cady had returned the favor and stood by Jeb when he'd done the unthinkable and bowed out on his wedding to Avalynne Stone, just moments before the ceremony was to start. With four hundred guests looking on in shock, Jeb had called off the ceremony, then made matters worse by refusing to offer any explanation other than that he'd decided commitment wasn't for him.

Neither the Stones nor the McCabes had ever forgiven him.

Although strangely enough, Avalynne had. Every time the former prom queen returned to Laramie—and she managed to visit there at least four times a year—she made time to see Jeb privately. And the two seemed to be getting along as well as ever.

Which was another fact no one could understand.

What kind of woman, Cady wondered, continued to have fond feelings for the restless cowboy who had publicly jilted her? And what about her ex? Was it possible Jeb harbored regrets about what he had done to Avalynne, and that was the real reason he refused to get serious about anyone, even ten years out?

It wasn't that he didn't date. He was always squiring women around to this event or that, but he was never with anyone he could get serious about.

Whereas it seemed, until recently anyway, Cady herself was always going out with potential Mr. Rights who turned out to be Mr. Wrongs.

Tired of that, she had focused on starting a family.

Now maybe it was finally happening.… And she was lucky enough to have Jeb right by her side, providing moral support the way she had once provided it to him.

Twenty minutes later, Cady and Jeb arrived at the Stork Agency residence in northwest Houston. They checked in at the front desk and were escorted to a small private courtyard.

A pretty young teenager with dark hair and eyes

stepped out of the dormitory. The petite seventeen-year-old was clearly in her last trimester.

Introductions were made by the staff counselor.

"So are you Cady's boyfriend?" Tina Matthews asked Jeb curiously.

Cady could imagine why the young woman would want that to be the case. Jeb wasn't just kind and easygoing. He was six foot three inches tall, with the broad shouldered, muscular build of a man who made his living riding horses and working cattle. A Texas cowboy through and through, he had thick, sandy-brown hair, blue-gray eyes and a ruggedly handsome face.

"Jeb is an old and trusted friend," Cady explained.

Tina fiddled with the notebook in her hands as she took him in from head to toe, studying the fit of his neatly pressed tan shirt and jeans, the smooth leather of his custom boots.

No doubt about it, Cady thought, Jeb looked as inherently masculine as he smelled—like leather and soap and the warm Texas sun.

"Then how come you're here—if you're just a friend?" the pregnant teen persisted.

Because I needed him, Cady thought to herself. *I can't say why, exactly, I just did.*

Jeb shrugged lazily. "Moral support," he said. "This is a big deal." He reached over and squeezed Cady's hand, before turning back to Tina. With a blast of McCabe charm, he added, "Cady was feeling a little nervous."

She wouldn't have admitted that. She didn't want to appear weak or unprepared in any respect in this situation. But it turned out to be the right thing to reveal.

Tina flashed a weak smile, as some of the tension left her pregnant form. "I'm nervous, too." Her gaze suddenly wise beyond her years, she raked her teeth across her lower lip. "I guess you know another couple was set to adopt my baby, but they backed out a few days ago."

Bolstered by Jeb's steady presence, Cady asked, "Do you know why?"

The teen sighed, her disappointment evident. "They decided adoption wasn't for them."

What a letdown that must have been, Cady thought compassionately. She leaned forward. "I'm sorry."

Tina nodded, accepting her sympathy. "Fortunately, there is no shortage of people wanting to adopt a newborn baby. I met with two other married couples this morning, and I'm meeting another couple—who live together but aren't married—this afternoon."

Cady hadn't realized this was a competition. Out of the corner of her eye, she could see Jeb's expression and tell he was equally surprised. She searched the girl's face. "Is it important to you that your baby be brought up by two parents?"

"Initially, I thought so, but then I saw your picture with your profile, and you looked so nice..." Tina shrugged and continued frankly, "I liked the fact that you grew up in a small town, same as me, but then moved to the city and built a successful career all on your own, like I want to do someday. I figured since you and I have so much in common, that might be good for my little girl, too."

A poignant silence fell. Cady didn't look at Jeb, but she could feel his concern.

"I wanted to keep my baby," Tina went on eventually, "but my parents were so embarrassed and upset, it just wasn't going to be an option."

Yet if she were just a year or so older, it would be, Cady thought, because Tina would be eighteen, and technically old enough to be out on her own.

Determined to understand, she asked gently, "How do they feel now?"

"Relieved, that I'm going to be able to put this behind me and go back to school and on to college and stuff." Tina stood and began to pace, rubbing her tummy as she moved. "They're also glad it's going to be an open adoption, so we'll know how my baby is doing, where she's growing up and all. Because they kind of worried about that, too."

Cady couldn't imagine surrendering a baby for adoption. However, that didn't stop her from admiring Tina's strength. "I can understand how that would be a comfort," she said quietly. *Knowing where your child was and that she was okay, even if you weren't the one raising her.*

"What about the baby's father?" Jeb asked kindly.

Tina scowled. "Bud signed away his rights as soon as he heard. He didn't want any part of this—or me."

Jeb looked as if he wanted to read the kid the riot act. "That really sucks."

"Yeah, but at least he didn't make any promises he had no intention of keeping. We all knew from the beginning that he wasn't going to be around. That made things clearer for me." Tina turned back to Cady. "How come you aren't married and don't have kids of your own already?"

A valid question, Cady acknowledged. She gestured helplessly. "I've come close a couple of times, when I was younger."

Tina studied her. "What happened?"

She sighed. "I took the guys home. They met my really pretty older sister and fell for her."

Tina Matthews looked horrified.

Cady lifted a hand and set the record straight. "It wasn't Suki's fault. She had no interest in dating them, but the guys were really smitten, and so…that ended that. I bounced back by becoming really focused on my career. And now that I'm in a good place professionally, I want to have a family of my own."

Tina's eyes lit with approval. "And you want to adopt."

"Yes. I want to give a child who has no place to go a loving, caring home."

THAT WAS CADY, Jeb thought. Noble to the core, and not afraid of commitment of any kind. Whereas he… Hell, even sitting here felt a little overwhelming.

Oblivious to his mixed emotions, Tina asked Cady, "Have you ever had any practice taking care of kids? I mean…for more than a few hours at a time?"

"Actually, I haven't," Cady admitted, then rushed to add, "but—starting Saturday—I am going to be babysitting my three nephews for two weeks."

"Stop looking at me like that," she told Jeb minutes later, after they had concluded their initial interview, said goodbye to Tina and headed for the parking lot.

He shook his head and stopped beside his pickup truck. "Can't help it." He paused, still in shock. "You're really going to babysit all of your sister's children for two weeks?" The three boys, ages two, four and five, were a handful under the best of circumstances, even for their very capable parents.

Cady released an exasperated breath. Pink color

staining her cheeks, she rifled through her handbag for her car keys. "How else am I going to get the kind of hands-on, in-depth experience I need?"

Trying not to notice how pretty she looked with the late afternoon sunshine shimmering in her golden-brown hair, Jeb opened a door to let the hot air escape from the cab. "Maybe you should try two days before you attempt two weeks," he chided.

Cady stood in front of her sporty white Lexus, her expression as maddeningly inscrutable as her posture. "In a perfect world, I'd agree with you."

But the world wasn't perfect, Jeb thought, or else Cady would be having a baby of her own, the old-fashioned way, with the man she loved.

"Unfortunately," she continued, using the button on her keypad to open the sunroof as well as all four windows, "it's not possible if Suki wants to resurrect her career as a set designer and location scout on the new movie Hermann is producing."

Able to feel the pent-up summer heat streaming from both vehicles, Jeb put his hand beneath Cady's elbow and steered her to a patch of shade beneath a tree, along the landscaped berm behind their vehicles. "She's going back to work?"

Cady nodded, her voice rife with emotion. "This is a chance for them to work together on a project again—*and* spend some rare time alone. And since Suki's never been to Australia..." She paused, her love and admiration for her big sister evident. "I want her to do this."

Cady's generosity did not surprise Jeb. He knew how close the two sisters had become since their parents' death in an auto accident, ten years before. "I'm all for getting practical experience of any kind," he said in exasperation, "but has it occurred to you that there are three of them, and only *one* of you?"

She huffed. "My sister manages the three boys all the time."

"She's had six years of practice to work up to her current skill level," Jeb pointed out.

Cady made a face at him. "It's not like Suki and Hermann live on a ranch and I have to take care of cows or anything, too. It'll just be the kids," she countered stubbornly. "And the house."

Jeb folded his arms, not about to back down, either. "Which is out in the country, a good twenty minutes from town."

The smile that curved her soft voluptuous lips did not reach her brown eyes. "Luckily for me, as Suki and Hermann pointed out, you live just down the road, cowboy."

Aha. So this was why she wasn't alarmed by the task ahead of her, Jeb thought, a bit peeved that she'd made this mutual commitment without first consulting him! Although he had to admit he didn't mind the prospect of spending more time than usual with her....

"Only one small problem," he reminded her bluntly, making no effort to hide his skepticism over the wisdom of her actions. "I have even less experience babysitting kids than you do."

"So?" Mischief dueled with the unwarranted confidence in her gaze. "You're a McCabe."

A McCabe who has no plans to ever get married.

Silence fell between them. Jeb didn't know why it mattered so much, but he could tell that Cady really wanted his approval. On this, as well as the adoption... Although why that should be baffled him, too.

"What's the matter, cowboy?" Cady taunted, her amber eyes sparkling in indignation. She marched closer, propping her hands on her slender hips and inundating him with a whiff of citrus perfume. "Don't you think I can do it?"

The question was, why would she want to? Jeb wondered drily. Especially given the little time off she had from work.

Knowing better than to answer her query directly, however, he lifted his palm and said instead, "Now, now, don't get your knickers in a knot."

Cady made a face at him. "Charming, Jeb."

He leaned in closer, too. "I'm just saying three boys can be a handful. Three boys five and under....well, that's a real task." One he wasn't sure either one of them was up to, promises or not.

Chapter Two

"You can stop looking at your watch anytime now," Hank McCabe drawled during Saturday evening's poker game.

Holden McCabe dealt two cards, facedown, to each player. As serious as ever, he turned to Jeb. "I agree with our brother that you're worrying needlessly. Cady and her nephews are all right."

"Otherwise," their cousin Kurt concurred with a knowing smile, "Cady surely would have called you."

Jeb feigned interest in his hand, although the truth was he'd never played a worse game of Texas hold 'em in his life. "She should have called me anyway," he grumbled.

Good-natured chuckles abounded as the game continued.

"How many texts have you sent her?" Hank asked curiously when Kyle got up to replenish the bowls of nuts and pretzels.

Frowning, Jeb tossed in a chip that would keep him in the game. "Since this morning?" He shrugged as all three of his brothers and his twin cousins, Kyle and Kurt, looked his way. "Maybe four..." Or had it been five? All he knew was that none had provoked a response of any kind. And that wasn't like Cady. Usually, when he called or texted or emailed, she got back to him within the hour, if not sooner.

"My guess is she's probably busy with the kids," Kyle said, returning to the table.

Jeb helped himself to a fistful of peanuts. "Maybe."

Holden set three community cards faceup in the center of the table. "You really think she's in trouble?"

"Yeah," Jeb said, recalling what a handful Suki and Hermann's three boys were, under the best of circumstances. "I do."

Kurt lifted a brow. "Then what are you doing here?"

"You're right." Jeb folded. Then he grabbed his jacket and took off.

Fifteen minutes later, he turned his pickup into the driveway of Suki and Hermann's home. It was nearly ten-thirty, yet enough lights were blazing to make him glad he'd followed his hunch and decided to stop by, despite the late hour. Jeb got out of his truck and headed for the front door.

Cady answered his knock almost immediately.

Her hair was gathered in a messy knot on top of her head. Her linen shirt and jeans bore a colorful array of stains. She looked more tired and frazzled than he had ever seen her. Behind her was an even worse mess, one her elegant older sister and equally discerning brother-in-law never would have allowed.

Worse, she looked anything but happy to see him, a fact that was even more baffling.

"I thought you were playing cards tonight," she said.

Jeb sized her up and decided she was embarrassed to be in a situation clearly beyond her control.

He shrugged. "The game ended early." *For me, anyway.*

The real question was, how best to lighten the mood?

"What's been going on here—a demolition derby?" Playfully, he inclined his head at the disarray behind her. "In any case, I think I know who won."

Cady's scowl morphed into a rueful grin. "Very funny, cowboy." Sighing woefully, she ushered him into her sister's opulent home.

Toys were strewn everywhere. An antique tin vase had been upended on the hall console and water and cut flowers dripped off onto the beautiful wood floor. Several planters had also been knocked over, and dirt and leafy plants were scattered across the plush carpet.

"Where are the kids?"

Cady put a finger to her lips, then motioned for him to follow.

Behind the U-shaped ultrasuede sofa in the living room, all three little boys were sprawled in a heap on the floor, like a pile of puppies. Their arms and legs were entangled, blankets and stuffed animals tossed around them. "I was just getting ready to carry them to their beds. That is—" she looked at the trail of belongings leading up the staircase "—if I can clear a path."

He acknowledged her statement with a slight nod of his head, his gaze meeting hers. "May I be of assistance?"

She threw up her hands. "At this point, any and all help would be greatly appreciated."

Gracefully, Cady led the way upstairs.

The hall bath was another disaster. The tub had been

drained of water, but wet towels and dirty clothing still needed to be picked up.

"Let me guess." Jeb plucked a rubber duckie from atop a towel rack and a plastic dump truck from the window ledge. "They were using the bath toys as missiles."

Cady leaned over to gather up discarded shoes, giving him a fine view of her very nice derriere in the process. "It's a good thing they were all made of soft rubber." As she straightened, the neckline of her linen blouse gaped slightly, giving him another unexpected view, this time of soft golden skin and lace-covered curves.

She readjusted the heart-shaped pendant about her neck and her cheeks registered a pretty pink flush. "I lost count of how many times I got hit with them."

Jeb ignored the growing pressure at the front of his jeans. He bent, gathered up the rest of the bath playthings and deposited them in the wire basket on the edge of the tub.

He straightened, towering over Cady once again. Wishing she weren't so deliciously disheveled, he remarked mildly, "Sounds like they were giving you the business."

She propped a fist on her hip. "Let's just say they weren't too pleased their parents were taking a trip without them."

Gazing into her whiskey-colored eyes, Jeb pushed aside the sudden desire to kiss her. "I'm sure they'll settle down tomorrow."

Cady pivoted and strode out of the bathroom, into the hall. "From your lips to their ear—eeyow!" She tripped on a plastic cowboy and horse set and went flying forward. Jeb caught her before she lost her balance completely, and brought her back upright. "Whoa, there, cowgirl."

Still wobbly, she turned around to face him, tripping over yet another toy in the process and bumping up against his chest.

Jeb continued holding her, surprised at how soft and feminine and vibrantly alive she felt. How good she smelled. Like baby shampoo, kiddie bubble bath and woman... With effort, he shifted her slightly backward, so they were no longer touching from sternum to knee. "You okay?"

"Yes. Thanks," she murmured throatily. Gulping, she carefully extricated herself from his steadying grip, yet still looked startled.

Jeb understood why.

Friends for years, they had occasionally exchanged the quick glad-to-see-you embrace that was the full body equivalent of an air-kiss. But never one intimate enough to have her brush up against him in quite that way.

The contact had given him an immediate physical reaction not suitable for friends.

Thanking heaven she seemed not to have noticed the rigid press of his body against the fly of his jeans, he bent to pick up a handful of toys scattered across the hallway, and deposit them out of harm's way.

Cady did the same, until a path had been cleared to all three of the boys' rooms.

Beds turned down and ready for their young occupants, Cady and Jeb headed down the stairs and made their way to the living room.

They deftly disentangled a little boy from the heap. Cady found the appropriate blanket and stuffed animal.

Jeb carried the sleeping child upstairs. Together, they tucked the little one into bed.

And went down for the next.

When all three were sleeping snugly in their beds, Cady led Jeb back downstairs. Bypassing the front door, she headed for the kitchen, at the rear of the house. "Thanks for coming over."

Glad she wasn't kicking him out, Jeb followed her lazily. "I figured you needed help." His gaze tracked the strands of hair escaping their loose knot and falling over one ear. He returned his glance to her face. "Otherwise, you would have answered my text messages."

Cady reached up to undo the pins. She slid them onto the neckline of her blouse as her hair fell to her shoulders in loose, sexy waves. "Yeah," she agreed, combing the strands into place with her fingers. "It's been a crazy, crazy night."

Jeb figured he'd better concentrate on something else or he would end up putting the moves on her.

"I can see that." He glanced around the kitchen.

Four barely eaten dinners were still on the kitchen table. An equal amount of pasta, sauce and salad dotted the floor, cabinets, and walls.

Most of a box of cookies, however, and a whole quart of milk were gone.

Jeb helped himself to a chocolate chip cookie and handed the remaining one to Cady.

She brought out another carton of milk, set it on the counter, then reached for two glasses. "Can you believe I've been in charge of them for only six hours?" she lamented. "Suki and Hermann didn't leave for the airport until five."

Jeb bypassed the chance to say I told you so. "Well, the boys are asleep now."

And she still had the dishes to do.

He accepted the glass of milk she gave him, took a sip and studied her chagrined expression over the rim. "Want some help with the rest of the cleanup?"

Cady smiled with a mixture of gratitude and relief. "You really are a friend, McCabe."

And that was all she wanted him to be, Jeb reminded himself firmly. A friend.

Once again he forced himself to table his disappointment and abide by her wishes.

"What time are the kids supposed to be up tomorrow?" he asked.

Cady glanced at the wall clock, which registered a little past eleven and her lips formed a thoughtful line. "Suki said they are usually up at six. But maybe the boys will sleep in, since they went to bed so late."

"What do you have planned for the day?"

She wrinkled her nose. "I was going to take them to the nature center at Lake Nasworthy, maybe hike some of the trails, but now I wonder if that's such a good idea." Her breasts rose and fell as she released a soft sigh. "They weren't exactly 'good listeners' tonight."

An understatement if Jeb had ever heard one.

Trying not to worry how Cady would react, or what message she would take from it, if it turned out she couldn't handle the kids on her own, Jeb soothed, "I'm sure the boys will be fine once you settle in. In the meantime, why don't you bring them over to my place for lunch? All my rodeo stock is out at events, but I've got a couple of newborn calves they might like to see."

Cady perked up. "You sure?"

Jeb nodded, glad to be of service. "I've got a meeting in the morning, but after eleven or so, I'm all yours," he promised.

"IS EVERYTHING OKAY?" Suki asked the following morning.

Cady pressed the phone closer to her ear. Most of what she could hear from Suki's end of the connection was an annoyingly loud public address system. "Where are you?"

"Atlanta." Suki shouted to be heard above the airport din. "Hermann and I are about to get on our connecting flight to Sydney. We won't be able to call again until we get there, and that will be another twenty-five hours."

Cady didn't envy them their long flight.

"I wanted to make sure you all were doing all right before we left the country!" her sister added.

"Tell her everything's fine, Cady!" Hermann chimed in with husbandly impatience.

Cady ignored the bits of once fluffy, golden pancake now smashed into the tabletop, chairs and floor.

From behind her, Finn grabbed the plastic bottle of maple syrup and upended it. Giving him a reproving look, she reached for it. Grinning like the little jokester he was, he dashed off, sticky bottle clutched in his hands. He passed it to the waiting five-year-old Dalton, and together they headed for two-year-old Micah.

Cady gasped at the trail of syrup being left behind, then groaned as the three boys rounded the corner and darted up the stairs.

Suki responded with a mother's radar. "Cady…!"

"Everything is fine," she fibbed. *Or at least it will be,*

she amended silently, repeating the mini pep talk Jeb had given her the previous evening, *once I settle in.*

"You all have a safe flight now," she said cheerfully. "Call me when you get to Sydney!"

"Bye, Cady, and thanks again!" Hermann shouted.

A click signaled the end of the call.

Cady put down the phone and dashed in the direction the boys had gone.

It took everything she had, but an hour later, she had all three of them strapped into Suki's Escalade.

By eleven sharp, she was turning the SUV into Jeb's ranch.

He was standing in the drive, talking to a man Cady didn't recognize. The two came to some agreement and shook hands. The tall man waved at Cady, got into a pickup truck bearing the name of a San Angelo, Texas, ranching operation, and took off.

Jeb strode toward Cady and the boys.

Finn, Dalton and Micah let out whoops of delight. "It's Our Friend Jeb!" they yelled in unison, calling him by the name they had given him years before.

"Hi, fellas." Jeb opened the rear door and began letting the boys out of their safety belts and booster seats. He ignored the smears of syrup in their hair. "Glad you could come and see me today."

"Aunt Cady said we could see the baby cows!"

"You sure can." Jeb paused to give Cady a quick, officious hug that as usual managed to avoid the full body contact they'd accidentally experienced the evening before.

Telling herself it was relief, not disappointment she felt, she watched as he took Finn's and Dalton's hands.

Cady took Micah's, and they set off toward the closest pasture.

There, in the green grass, stood half a dozen baby calves, each about the size of a large dog. "How come they're all black except for their faces?" Dalton asked with a perplexed frown.

"Yeah, how come their faces are white?" Finn added, his small brow wrinkling in consternation.

"Cow," said Micah. He reached out to shyly touch one of the forty-pound baby calves. "Moooo."

Everyone laughed.

Micah looked up at them, his two-year-old face scrunched in bewilderment. "Cow," he repeated, as if no one had heard him correctly. *"Moooo."*

"Yes, that's a cow and it moos," Cady confirmed gently.

With Jeb's assistance, the two older boys petted the baby calves, too. "They're really kind of soft." Dalton ran a hand through one's silky coat.

"I think they like us," Finn noted, petting another.

Jeb smiled in agreement. "I think the baby calves like you fellas, too."

Cady's phone began to ring. She plucked it from her pants pocket and checked the caller ID screen. The Stork Adoption Agency. Her heart skipped a beat. She looked at Jeb. "I better get this."

"Go ahead." He waved her off. "I'll help the boys out of the pasture."

While he lifted them over the fence, she moved a short distance away. What the director had to say was both comforting and disturbing.

"Everything okay?" Jeb asked when she rejoined

him. The three boys romped ahead for the next part of the tour—the barn.

Glad that once again she had her friend there to lean on, Cady found solace in Jeb's blue-gray eyes. "Tina Matthews has narrowed it down to me and another couple. She has a few more questions for me and wants to set up a phone interview right away."

Jeb cast a glance at the boys, who were hopping around by the barn entrance waiting as ordered for the adults to catch up. He turned back to Cady. "Want me to watch the boys while you make the call?" Understanding colored his low tone.

Reassured by Jeb's calm, steady presence, Cady sagged in relief. "Thank you." There was so much on the line now. She was so close to getting a family of her own. She didn't want to blow it by giving the matter less than her full attention. "That would be so..."

Cady stopped dead in her tracks, realizing that once again the boys were misbehaving. "Oh, no," she murmured.

"Oh no is right." Jeb swore as a trio of high-pitched screams split the air.

Together, Cady and Jeb ran toward the sound.

JEB DIDN'T KNOW WHETHER to be irritated or amazed that the three boys had gotten into trouble so quickly.

They were lucky the heifer whose stall they had opened was a lot more interested in chewing her feed than in the three little tykes staring up at her and screaming their heads off in abject terror at the thousand pound, black-and-white mama cow.

"Hush, now." Jeb handed Micah to Cady, then scooped the older two boys up in his arms.

Figuring they'd had enough adventures for a while, he shut the stall door and led the way out of the barn. "You boys are all right."

Micah buried his face in Cady's shoulder and held on to her neck for dear life.

"Cow scared me," the toddler wailed between hysterical hiccups.

"I know she did, and it's my fault." Jeb shifted Finn and Dalton into a more comfortable position in his arms and carried them across the yard to his mission-style ranch house.

Aware this was something Cady could not have done alone, he opened the door and stepped inside.

"I should never have let you fellas take the lead," Jeb told the boys sternly. "This is a good lesson for all of us. When you're here, visiting, you-all need to stay with a grown-up. No more running on ahead of us. Ever." He paused to make his point. "A ranch can be a dangerous place." His expression serious, Jeb made prolonged eye contact with each of the children. "Got it?"

The older boys nodded wordlessly.

Gently, Jeb set them down on the red tile floor.

He reached for Micah.

The toddler went to him reluctantly.

Jeb cradled the child in his arms, surprised at how good—how right—it felt. The boy laced his own arms about Jeb's neck and laid his head against his shoulder, his tiny body sagging in relief at the tender, loving protection the cowboy offered.

Without warning, Jeb felt an unexpected pang of envy for all the people his age who had loving spouses and kids of their own.

But that was neither here nor there, when Cady had such an important call to make.

Wanting her to get everything she yearned for and more, he nodded at her officiously. "Go." Clasping her shoulder, he spun her in the direction of his study. "Shut the door and make your call."

She bit her lip and shot him an uncertain look, as if wondering if it was okay to leave him with all three boys, after the way they had just behaved.

Jeb lifted a staying hand. "I've got it covered," he promised, with a sober look meant to instill her with confidence.

Still she didn't move.

"I'll help the boys wash up and then we'll make lunch," he continued matter-of-factly. "You can join us when you're done."

And then, Jeb added silently to himself, *you and I are going to have the talk we should have had last night.*

IT WAS A GOOD HALF HOUR before Cady emerged from the study and went in search of Jeb and the boys. She found them in the family room, at the back of the house. Jeb was working in the adjacent kitchen. Shirtsleeves rolled up to just below the elbow, he looked handsome and at ease as he cut up an apple and divided the thin crescents into three bowls.

Dalton, Finn, and Micah were sitting side by side on Jeb's leather sofa, munching sandwiches and chips and sipping from juice boxes.

All three boys were thoroughly immersed in a TV program. They looked so calm and content and perfectly at home in his bachelor lair that it put her own efforts to care for them to shame.

Trying not to feel too bad about that, Cady sighed.

Jeb caught her eye and flashed her a sexy smile. "The Berenstain Bears," he explained. He delivered the fruit to the boys, then came back to her. "Kurt and Paige recommended it. Said it's very soothing and works wonders for their triplets when they need to chill out. And as an added bonus—" Jeb leaned down to murmur in her ear "—there's a valuable moral in every story."

Suki and Hermann would appreciate that, too. Cady nodded, letting Jeb know she approved.

"It was a good idea. The kids have some of their storybooks in their rooms," she replied quietly, being careful not to disturb the unexpected tranquility surrounding her three nephews.

He stepped back, putting the usual physical distance between them. His gaze slid past the hollow of her throat to her lips, then her eyes. "How did your call with Tina Matthews go?" Hand on her elbow, he ushered her past the breakfast room to the kitchen.

As always, Jeb's ultramasculine presence, the brisk sun-warmed-leather scent of him, made her feel protected and intensely aware.

In an attempt to regain her equilibrium, she kept her distance as they reached the kitchen. She saw he'd already set out plates on the island bar and filled two glasses with ice and her favorite peach tea.

She picked one up and took a sip. "Fine." Briefly, she lowered her glance, adding uncertainly, "I think." It was so hard to tell in a situation that was this tricky to navigate.

Jeb gazed at her gently. "When is she going to make up her mind?"

Trying not to get ahead of herself and celebrate

something that might not happen, after all, Cady cleared her throat and said, "Sometime in the next couple of days."

Aware that her throat felt parched, and she was very much in need of a hug, Cady took another longer drink.

Swallowing, she met Jeb's eyes and found the kind of comfort only he could give. "The director said they would let me know as soon as Tina decides."

The corners of his lips turned up in a hopeful smile. He shifted his brows encouragingly and patted her on the shoulder. "You're getting closer to becoming a mom."

Despite her earlier decision to remain cautious, Cady found his optimism contagious. "I hope so."

"Which reminds me." He brought a plate of ham and cheese sandwiches out of the fridge and set them on the counter next to the peanut butter and jelly. He gestured, indicating she should pull up a stool and help herself. "Paige and Kurt also gave me the name of a San Angelo service where they got their nanny. Apparently the agency will arrange short-term gigs as well as long-term placements."

Cady glanced up from the lunch he had prepared to stare at him, confused. "Why would I need a nanny? I haven't even been chosen for adoption yet."

"I was talking about now, for the boys," Jeb interjected amiably.

Cady's temper flared. She didn't need to call in professionals! "Just because *you* couldn't last a week…" she countered, incensed that he apparently thought her totally incompetent when it came to caring for her three nephews. So she'd had an unexpectedly rocky start. So what? He'd had to use TV and the soothing entertainment of the Berenstain Bears to rein them in!

Jeb braced his hands on his hips as if for battle. "How long I could hang in here is hardly the point," Jeb retorted, looking her straight in the eye. "Although, for the record, I could easily weather two weeks."

Which, coincidentally, was exactly the amount of time she was staying in Laramie.

Narrowing her gaze, Cady slid right back off the stool and stomped closer. "Want to bet?"

"Yes." Jeb studied her just as contentiously. "As a matter of fact, Cady," he drawled, grinning complacently, "I do."

Chapter Three

Cady blinked, unable to believe what Jeb had just said. "Are you serious?"

An arrogant smile crossed his handsome face. "Have you ever known me not to be, when it comes to a wager?"

She stared at him, wondering how he could continue to look so cool and confident when she felt so frazzled. She stepped closer. "Better be careful," she taunted lightly. "I might just take you up on that."

And then what would the man famous for his lack of commitment do?

Jeb shrugged his broad shoulders. "Why wouldn't you?" he challenged in a husky voice that drew her even deeper into their sudden battle of wits and wills.

"Unless—" Jeb snapped his fingers, as illumination hit "—you're afraid of being shown up?"

She was afraid, all right, but not of that.

Struggling not to notice how good Jeb looked, with the blue chambray shirt bringing out the blue-gray of his eyes, Cady fastened her gaze on the strong column of his throat and the tufts of sandy hair visible in the open collar of his shirt.

When she felt composed enough, she returned her

glance to his. "Surely," she commented wryly, "you jest."

His eyes lit up the way they always did when he knew he'd gotten under her skin, and hence earned her full attention. He leaned closer, his warm breath whispering across her ear. "We've got to face facts here, Cady. I'm in charge and the boys are perfect little angels."

With a hand to his chest, she pushed him back, knowing she had to maintain her physical—and emotional—distance in order to make her point. She flashed him a sassy smile she couldn't really begin to feel, considering the ineptitude she had demonstrated in the parenting department thus far. "They behaved for me, too, for the first hour or so." She regarded him with a deliberately provoking manner, aware that Jeb—like everyone else she knew—harbored some doubts about the advisability of her plan to adopt a baby as a single mom. "It was after that when it got tough. But clearly," she continued sarcastically, "you don't think the same thing would happen to you."

"Honestly?" Jeb rubbed his palm across his closely shaved jaw, then lazily dropped his hand again. "No. As a matter of fact, I don't."

"Okay, then, Mr. Smarty Pants," Cady agreed with a sharp look, her temper igniting. "We're on."

He chuckled, his eyes gleaming wickedly in anticipation. "Or we will be," he promised huskily, "as soon as we decide the stakes of our wager."

"Nothing pedestrian," she warned.

He squinted in speculation. He obviously didn't want to be bored, either. "Agreed."

It was her turn to snap her fingers. "Then I know what I want," Cady exclaimed, as inspiration hit. She folded her arms in front of her and rocked back on her heels. "If I win, you have to tell me why you broke up with Avalynne Stone just minutes before she was supposed to walk down the aisle to marry you."

Jeb's gaze swept over Cady's form-fitting ranch jeans, red cotton shirt, and boots, before returning, ever so slowly and deliberately, to her face. "You already know the answer to that," he said stoically, with a look that would have warned off a lesser woman.

Cady squinted right back at him, glad the conversation had shifted from her temporary ineptitude in the mothering department to his continuing incapability in the commitment arena. "I know what you said at the time," she told him sweetly, not sure why this had always bothered her so, just knowing that deep down it did. The only difference was she had never before had the nerve, or the opportunity, to bring it up.

She continued holding his laserlike gaze. "And guess what, cowboy? I don't buy it."

Typical bravura replaced the fleeting emotion reflected on his face. He shrugged, all strong implacable male. "I don't see why not." He folded his arms, mirroring her posture, then rocked forward on the toes of his boots and lowered his face to hers until they were practically nose to nose. "I'm not the first guy to decide I didn't want to be shackled to someone else for the rest of my life."

Cady didn't like the conquering look in his eyes, or the presumption in his low tone that said as far as he was concerned this was all a moot point, because he had already won their bet. Determined not to let him shut her out the way he shut out everyone else when this subject came up, she murmured, "And yet…you were upset for months afterward." Not exactly the response of a guy who had gotten exactly what he wanted, come hell or high water, she thought.

Jeb came even closer, the warmth of his breath ghosting over her temples. "With good reason," he admitted sagely. "Everyone was ticked off at me." He paused, lifting an eyebrow. "My parents still haven't forgiven me."

Which hadn't been the worst of it, Cady recalled. "Avalynne's parents sued you for the expense of the wedding." He had owed them almost fifty thousand dollars!

For a moment, Jeb went very still. Then he shrugged, offhand as ever. "They felt justified."

What a mess that had been, she mused. She adapted an equally nonchalant posture. "So you paid."

He shrugged again. "It seemed like the gentlemanly thing to do under the circumstances."

Determined not to put herself in an emotionally vulnerable position with him, Cady observed with a slight twinge of jealousy, "And yet you and Avalynne Stone remain close."

Jeb exhaled, looking irritated again. "I don't know why that's so surprising to everyone," he groused. "She and I have been friends our whole lives."

Still…

Cady's feminine instincts were on full alert. "Most women wouldn't forgive being embarrassed and humiliated in front of the entire town," she pointed out, wishing she wasn't so physically attracted to Jeb.

He studied her, as if trying to decide how much further he wanted this discussion to go.

She flushed under his intense scrutiny. It was

disconcerting having him trying to figure out what was on her mind and in her heart, too.

"Avalynne Stone is not like most women," he said finally.

"Clearly," Cady stated, relieved to have the conversation going forward once again.

"Has she shown any signs of settling down yet—in any regard?" Cady asked curiously.

Jeb exhaled with a weariness that seemed to come straight from his soul. He knew full well Avalynne's rootlessness was blamed on him. "She likes to travel."

An understatement, if Cady had ever heard one. "I guess so, since she's backpacked and sailed around the world—what, three times now?—trying to 'find herself'."

"She's an artist. She goes wherever she can find the inspiration she needs to paint," Jeb said brusquely. "And why does any of this matter to you?"

Because, Cady thought to herself, this was the one thing about Jeb McCabe that had never made sense to her, the one thing that stood between the two of them becoming really close. Until she knew why he'd abruptly behaved so dishonorably, she would never really understand him.

And for reasons she chose not to analyze, she wanted to know Jeb as completely as it was possible to know another human being.

Stubbornly allowing her motivation to remain as mysterious as his, she said offhandedly, "I guess I'm just insatiably curious."

And left it at that.

Jeb surveyed her a moment longer, an indefinable emotion flickering in his eyes. Finally, he relented.

"Okay, if you win, I'll tell you everything Avalynne and I said to each other that day in the church."

He angled a thumb at his chest. "But if I win, you have to not only promise never to bring up the Avalynne Stone incident again, but help me figure out a way to put the whole fiasco behind me once and for all."

His proposal was tantalizing in its intimacy. Still, Cady found herself getting defensive. "You make it sound like I bring it up all the time," she said. "I don't."

"Of course not." The corners of Jeb's lips slanted downward. "You and everyone else I know just can't help thinking about it every time Avalynne comes to town to visit her folks, or when the topic of weddings, broken engagements or embarrassing life incidents comes up." He paused, shook his head. "It's always there, Cady. The memory of what should have happened and didn't."

She couldn't say she was sad that Jeb and Avalynne hadn't married. Although the two had made a handsome couple, she'd never thought they belonged together, long term.

Everyone else, however, had.

She shrugged and held out a hand to seal the deal. The warmth of his clasp had her pulse racing.

"All right, if I lose, I'll stop asking, and I'll help you get your reputation with the ladies back. So that if you ever do change your mind," Cady teased, "and decide to pick a woman and settle down, it won't be as the heart-breaker you've been deemed for the last ten years."

"Do Mom and Dad know you're planning on playing house with Cady and her three nephews for the next two weeks?" Emily asked Jeb several hours later.

Beginning to regret his decision to stop by the Daybreak Café to pick up a day's worth of meals to go, Jeb regarded his little sister—the proprietress of the establishment—with a great deal more patience than he felt. "It's a bet, Emily."

She scooped fruit salad, bursting with summer melon, peaches and berries, into takeout containers. "A bet that will have you sleeping under the same roof as her for the next two weeks!"

Jeb pushed away the image of Cady in her pajamas. So she was sexy as all get-out, and mysterious in all the ways that drew him in. The two of them were just friends.

He fitted the lids on the fruit salad containers with more care than necessary. "Are you saying I won't be able to restrain myself?"

Emily spooned macaroni and cheese into a foil pan, then tossed him a knowing look. "Are you saying you aren't physically attracted to her? Because from what I've seen—" she made an impish face "—there are definitely sparks between you two."

Jeb thought about Cady's soft hair and softer skin.

"Sparks of friendship…" he allowed, reminding himself sternly that this was a road Cady had decided a long time ago not to venture down.

"Or something more."

Jeb didn't indulge in wishful thinking. Especially when it could end up breaking his heart.

He put the containers into sacks. "We're going to have three chaperones, remember?"

Emily scoffed and planted a hand on the side of her head as if she'd just had a lightbulb moment. "You're right. I'm sure there will be zero opportunity to get romantic."

He mimed a playful swat to her arm. "Enough, Emily."

She merely grinned, as if she knew something he didn't.

And maybe his baby sis did, Jeb thought as he drove back out to Suki and Hermann's place. Fifteen months prior, the feisty and irrepressible Emily had hooked up with an equally independent horse whisperer. Their obviously feigned flirtation soon turned into the real thing. The love they found had tamed their wild hearts. They'd since married and settled blissfully into a life together. And made it all look a lot easier than watching over three little kids.

Who were all at this very moment, standing in the front yard. Little Micah had his head tilted skyward and was screaming at the top of his lungs. Finn and Dalton, his towheaded older brothers, stood beside him, also looking up, their hands pressed over their ears.

Where was Cady? Jeb wondered uneasily as he climbed out of his pickup.

And then he saw her, bare-legged and barefoot, halfway up a huge live oak tree.

She had changed since he had last seen her, and was now clad in a pair of trim khaki shorts and a figure-hugging pink T-shirt. Her golden-brown hair had been up swept haphazardly and was pinned on top of her head.

With one foot on the trunk some ten feet in the air, another braced on a limb, she was studying the far branches when Jeb strode over and scooped Micah into his arms.

"Hush now," Jeb told the shrieking child, who was so astounded by his arrival that he did momentarily stop sobbing.

Jeb frowned at Cady. "What the…uh, what are you doing up there?" he demanded, censoring himself just in time.

She huffed and looked down at him. "Rescuing Curious George and yellow blankie," she said.

Jeb followed her gaze.

Sure enough, both were caught on a branch.

The culprits who had somehow managed to throw the beloved objects up there, lingered guiltily beside their baby brother.

"Cady, come down from there," Jeb ordered. "I'll do it."

She wrinkled her brow, insulted. "No way."

He continued patting Micah on the back. "It's dangerous, Cady!"

"If you don't know what you're doing, I agree, it would be," she said glibly. "As it happens, however, I am an expert tree climber. Always have been, always will be."

This was not the example to be setting for those boys, Jeb thought, or an argument to be held in front of them. "Cady…"

Ignoring his entreaty, she held on to the trunk with her right arm and reached out with her left, her fingers coming just short of her goal. Scowling, she straightened and tried again, this time using her foot.

The three boys stared upward, clearly mesmerized by their aunt's derring-do.

"Cady," Jeb warned again, "I mean it…."

Ignoring him, she held the trunk with both arms,

shifted her weight on the limb and tried again, with her other foot extended. This time she made contact. A nudge, then another, and both Curious George and yellow blankie fluttered through the leaves to the ground.

"My monkey and blankie!" Micah shouted gleefully.

Jeb set the toddler down to retrieve them.

Smiling triumphantly, Cady pulled herself back to the trunk and made her way carefully down it, her shorts riding up her long lissome thighs. When she was within reach, Jeb hooked his hands around her waist and swung her the rest of the way down to the ground.

Her cheeks were bright pink with exertion as their gazes meshed. Just that swiftly, Jeb felt the zing of attraction he did not want to feel when they were under the same roof.

Cady turned to the older boys. "All right, you two. Tell your little brother you're sorry."

"We were just joking around," Finn protested.

"Yeah, trying to make George and blankie fly," Dalton agreed.

Cady looked down her nose in reproof. "If you want to do experiments like that, you do them with your own toys. Not his."

"How come?" Finn challenged, while Dalton pouted.

"Because when you took his toys from him, you upset Micah and made him cry. And that's not nice," she scolded.

Finn and Dalton regarded their younger brother with a mixture of scorn and regret.

"Sorry," they said in unison.

Cady continued regarding them sternly. "It better not happen again. Got it?"

They sighed once more. "Got it," they grumbled.

Micah sank onto the thick grass, his face buried in his blanket, his monkey in his arms.

Admiring the way Cady had taken charge of the situation and restored order, Jeb said, "I brought some food from town. Maybe Finn and Dalton can help me bring it in."

"Good idea." Cady slid her flip-flops on, picked up Micah and carried him and his treasures toward the house.

"Why were you boys teasing your brother?" Jeb asked, picking up where she had left off.

"I dunno." Finn shrugged.

"Because we like to?" Dalton guessed.

"What do your mom and dad say when that happens?"

"We get a time out," Finn answered. "Are you going to give us a time out?"

Jeb set a hand on a shoulder of each and guided them to his truck. "I'm going to put you to work instead."

Jeb gave both the boys a small bag to carry and brought the rest into the house. Cady was in the kitchen, cleaning up. Micah was sitting at the table, molding modeling clay into shapes. It was a sweet domestic scene, and Jeb found himself oddly touched. Cady was going to make a great mom.

The only problem was, he wasn't going to be a part of it. Not as he was today, he realized in regret.

"Thanks for doing this," she told him.

Jeb forced himself to stop the wishful thinking. "No problem."

Finn and Dalton went over to the table and looked at Micah. "Can we play, too?"

Cady and Jeb waited to see what Micah would do. His lower lip shot out petulantly as he looked up at his hopeful brothers. "Okay," he said finally, and Finn and Dalton happily joined him.

With peace restored, Cady glanced at her watch, then Jeb. "Do you want to bring the rest of your things in?"

He tore his gaze away from her lips. This was no time to be thinking about kissing her. Maybe he should give her a way out of all this togetherness. Especially given the ardent direction of his thoughts...

He frowned. "Do you have a place for me to sleep? Because if not, I could just leave late and come back early. You know, be here for everything important with the tykes."

Jeb had half expected his suggestion to be met with relief, now that she'd had time to think about how intimate a proposition residing under the same roof would be.

Instead, Cady's jaw dropped and her eyes blazed with indignation. "I can't believe it. You're already trying to get out of our bet!"

Holding her gaze, he shook his head and lounged back against the counter. "No...I'm not."

She closed in on him, her cheeks a riot of color. "Yes, you are."

It was all Jeb could do not to take her in his arms. Undo that clip, run his hands through her lush hair, feeling it's softness....

He swallowed, pushing the urge away, then called upon his younger sister's words. "I just don't want

you—or anyone else in the community—to think I'm
in this to 'play house'...."

Because that would be the obvious assumption to
make. That he and Cady were if not already sleeping
together, then well on their way to a scandalous affair.
And he didn't want to see her reputation in Laramie
reduced to the level of his.

The activity at the kitchen table stopped. Three heads
lifted and turned in their direction. "Who's playing
house?" Dalton piped up.

"No one," Cady said firmly, suddenly unable to meet
Jeb's gaze.

Wrapping her hand around his elbow, she guided him
down the hall toward the front of the house. As soon as
they were safely out of earshot, she dropped her hand
and looked up at him. "I know I don't have to worry,"
she said sincerely. "Because I know you're not the kind
of guy who would take advantage of this situation and
try to get me into bed."

"Is Our Friend Jeb going to have a sleepover with you,
Aunt Cady?" Finn asked as he climbed into the bathtub,
along with his brothers.

Thankful that Jeb had gone to the linen closet to get
towels, and wasn't there to see her blush, Cady poured
shampoo on her palm and lathered it into the hair of all
three boys. "No, honey, Jeb is going to be sleeping in
the other guest room."

"How come?" Dalton played with the froth of bubbles
floating on the water.

She turned on the hand-sprayer and adjusted the
temperature to lukewarm. "Because he needs his privacy." *And I need mine, to keep myself from conjuring*

up any romantic fantasies that will never, under any circumstances, come true. Just because Jeb is sexy as all get-out, just because I've had a secret crush on him for what seems forever, does not mean he will suddenly turn into the marrying kind.

And with her set to adopt a child as soon as possible, Cady knew she only had room in her life for a serious-minded man who was ready to settle down.

So like it or not, Jeb was definitely out of the running for anything more than friendship.

As was she.

Finn tipped his head back while she rinsed his hair. "Is Our Friend Jeb your boyfriend?" he asked curiously.

Finished, Cady handed Finn a dry washcloth to blot his face. "No. He's my *friend*." Emphasis on the platonic.

Dalton closed his eyes while Cady rinsed the soap from his hair, too. "Well, maybe he should be, because Momma told Daddy that you need to get a boyfriend so you won't turn into an old maid."

Jeb chose that moment to walk back in, stack of towels in hand. He looked at Cady in abject sympathy and mouthed, "Nice."

She agreed.

Although she was sure the sentiment expressed by her older sister was well-meant—and not for little ears.

Suki and Hermann just wanted to see her happy.

And to them, that meant married happily ever after, like they were.

"What's an old maid?" Micah sailed a toy boat across the water.

Being careful not to get any water in his eyes, Cady

rinsed his hair in turn. "A woman who never married before she got old."

"You are old, Aunt Cady," Finn pointed out helpfully. "You're going to be sixty-four on your birthday."

She winced at just the thought, while Jeb jumped in, and corrected, "That's thirty-four, fellas, and gentlemen *never* discuss a lady's age."

Dalton struggled to understand. "How come?" He climbed out of the tub, and his brothers followed suit.

Jeb wrapped the oldest boy in the towel and watched as Cady did the same with her other nephews. "It's not polite."

"How come?" Finn echoed.

After Cady finished drying Micah and Finn, she got out the pajamas. "Because grown-ups don't like to think about getting old."

"Why not?" Micah prodded, while he and his brothers got dressed for bed.

Cady drained the water from the tub and hung up the damp towels. "It reminds them of all the things they haven't gotten done that they want to."

"Okay, fellas, that's enough questions for Aunt Cady," Jeb said as he ran a comb through Dalton's hair and then got to work on the other two boys.

"Are you going to have a cake on your birthday, Aunt Cady?" Finn asked, clearly not getting the hint.

She sighed and layered toothpaste on all three brushes. "Yes, I'll have cake."

"Can we have some?" Dalton asked.

"On my birthday, yes, you can."

Jeb handed out three small paper cups of water. "Rinse and spit, guys. Then time for bed."

"Are you going to read us stories?" Finn asked.

Trying not to think how easily she and Jeb meshed in the mommy and daddy roles, Cady nodded. "Jeb is going to read to you two older boys, and then sit in your room with you until you fall asleep. And I'm going to read to Micah and rock him to sleep."

"Will you be here in the morning when we wake up?" Dalton asked Jeb.

He nodded, looking as happy and content as Cady felt at that moment. "I will," he said in a soft, sure voice that sent ripples up and down Cady's spine.

AN HOUR LATER, when all three boys were fast asleep in their beds, Cady joined Jeb in the family room. He had taken off his boots and kicked back in the daddy chair, his feet propped on the ottoman. His sandy-brown hair was delectably rumpled, and the shadow of evening beard lined his handsome face.

Cady could only wonder how he would look come morning, when he tumbled out of bed, dressed in who knew what.

Her guess was he'd appear even more masculine, sexy and relaxed.

And that could mean the kind of trouble neither of them needed if they were to end this bet with their friendship intact.

Which was why she needed to do whatever she could to diffuse the false intimacy of the situation.

"Are you sure being here in the morning, first thing, is a promise you can keep?" Cady walked around, shutting blinds and turning on extra lights, despite the fact it wasn't entirely dark outside yet. "Don't you have to take care of your herd or something?" Wouldn't it be better if he joined them later, say, after both had showered and donned the day's armor?

He lowered the newspaper he had been reading. "I do, but that can be done at any time during the day, and I can take you and the boys with me during chore time." He shrugged laconically. "At least that was the plan...."

Silence fell. Cady became aware it was only eight o'clock. The night loomed ahead of them, like a pitfall to be avoided.

"We did pretty well this evening," Jeb continued, studying her as if trying to read her sudden change of mood.

Cady nodded and continued to roam the room self-consciously, straightening a book here, a pillow there. "That's because there were two of us to ride herd on them," she said, feeling his eyes trail over her from head to toe.

Just because she was attracted to Jeb didn't mean he was attracted to her...

"And," she continued in the most even voice she could manage, "it probably felt more normal to them, having both a mom and a dad here at dinner and bath time. Suki and Hermann are a really good team."

Jeb's eyes gleamed with self-effacing humor. "We aren't so bad, either, Cady."

No, they weren't.

Still, she warned herself not to read too much into that, any more than she should read anything into Jeb's apparent contentment being with her and the boys this evening. "Beginner's luck."

"Maybe," he allowed.

And maybe, he seemed to be thinking but didn't say, *it's more than that.*

Or was that wishful thinking on her part? Cady wondered, feeling even more off balance and ill at ease. Which was ridiculous, really. She and Jeb had been alone together plenty of times. Maybe they hadn't spent the night together under the same roof, but—

Her phone rang.

Jeb's brow furrowed. "Suki again?"

Cady shook her head. "They won't be landing until tomorrow morning. It's probably work, wanting to know if I've had time to look at the male spokesmodel candidates for the Hanover Horseshoe campaign yet."

But it wasn't work, Cady discovered as she retrieved her phone and glanced at her caller ID. It was someone much more important.

And, as it happened, the news was all she could have wished for.

"Well?" Jeb said, minutes later, when Cady ended the conversation and finally put down the phone.

He got to his feet and came toward her. "What happened?" he asked with concern. "Why are you crying?"

"Because," Cady gulped, unsure whether she was more happy or shell-shocked. All she knew was that she couldn't have had better news. She drew a stabilizing breath and looked deep into Jeb's eyes. "I'm finally getting what I have wanted for a very long time."

Recognition dawned. "The baby," he said hoarsely.

"Yes!" She did a brief, ecstatic happy dance. "Jeb! Tina Matthews chose me!"

Jeb wrapped Cady in a hug. She hugged him back hard, joy flowing through her.

It was only when she drew back and looked up into his face that things changed. The happiness morphed into something else, something stronger and far more life-altering. And in that instant, as their eyes locked and their breathing hitched, even before Jeb's head lowered inevitably toward hers, Cady knew that he felt it, too.

Chapter Four

Jeb had promised himself he wouldn't kiss Cady or let things get out of hand, but when she launched herself against him without reservation, all previous declarations were off.

All he knew was how she felt—soft and warm and right. All he knew was how she tasted—sweet and hot and womanly.

Had she not surrendered so completely to the pressure of his mouth against hers, had she not opened her lips and tangled her tongue with his, maybe the kiss would have been quick and efficient…and a heck of a lot easier to walk away from.

Instead, she went up on tiptoe, wreathing her arms around his neck, pressing her whole body against his. Softness to hardness, woman to man… It was, Jeb thought as he continued kissing Cady with everything he had, as if the wall around her heart had lowered just enough to let him in.

He was beginning to let his guard down, too, when Cady came abruptly to her senses, broke off their kiss and pulled away.

Tense seconds passed as they stared at each other in confusion.

Cady flushed. She pressed a hand against her trembling lips and drew a deep, bolstering breath. "I am... so sorry..." she said.

"I'm not." Now that the door had been eased open, Jeb wasn't about to back down. He looked her straight in the eye, unwilling to tell anything but the truth. "That kiss was hot."

She grinned sheepishly. "Tell me about it. But that doesn't make it right. I used you just now..."

"Used me?" Jeb echoed in stunned amazement.

Running both hands through her hair, she backed away, putting even more distance between them. "Yes. I mean..." She paused and bit her lip. "I had all this emotion with nowhere to put it...."

He favored her with a deadpan look and finished her thought for her. "So you planted one on me."

Another shimmer of tension floated between them. "I don't want to do anything that would ever harm our friendship."

"I don't, either." That did not mean a door hadn't been opened....

She scowled, her frustration apparent. "Hooking up... would ruin everything."

Resisting the urge to take her right back into his arms and swiftly prove otherwise, he inclined his head and asked, "Was that what we were about to do?"

Her elegant brows arched in wordless censure. "We're both adults," she reminded him tersely. She paced back and forth, her hands knotted in front of her. "We know where passion like that—if left unchecked—leads."

Jeb could not deny the yearning building inside him, any more than he could refute the pressure in his groin. "And you don't want to go there."

Cady paused, her brief hesitation telling him more than any of her denials. "I have a lot going on right now. Three children to take care of. Work to do. An adoption to plan for…"

It was easy to see why she felt overwhelmed in the moment. "You're right," he agreed gently. "The timing is lousy."

Her cheeks pinkening, Cady swallowed. "So we're agreed?" She searched his eyes. "No more kissing?"

Jeb gave her the reassurance she obviously craved. "I'll be the perfect gentleman the rest of the evening. I promise."

After that, once things settled down, was a different matter entirely.

WITH THE KIDS ASLEEP and the evening dragging out, Cady decided to catch up on her email.

While she set up her laptop computer in the family room, Jeb drove down the road to his ranch, checked on his herd and brought back his own laptop and a backpack full of files.

He had obviously showered and changed while at home, and the fragrance of soap and shaving cream clung to his skin. His still-damp hair curled at the nape of his neck.

"I didn't realize ranching required so much paperwork," Cady murmured, ignoring the way her heart skittered at his nearness.

He stopped setting up long enough to give her a warm smile. "Normally, it doesn't, but I'm in the process of getting out of rodeo stock boarding."

Here he went again, Cady thought unhappily, recalling that Jeb never stayed with anything for long.

Two years into agricultural college, he'd dropped out, hit the rodeo circuit and become a star. After several years, he grew bored with competing and went on to a second university, this time with a business major. During that time, he invested his winnings in the stock market, graduated with a degree in finance and attempted to marry Avalynne, before changing his mind about that and leaving his fiancée literally stranded at the altar. The lawsuit from her family followed but was swiftly settled out of court, and Jeb left Laramie County once again. A stint working as a broker in Dallas combined with his investment income earned him enough money to purchase a ranch. Bored with city life, he returned to Laramie, bought property and christened it the Flying M Ranch and then began boarding and transporting rodeo stock for friends. Now, apparently, he was tired of that, too.

But was it a good business decision to just get out? Cady wondered. "I thought that was what paid your mortgage."

"It's what has paid off the mortgage on my ranch," Jeb corrected with a smile. "Now that I own my land and house outright, I want to expand my breeding into a much larger operation. I've got plenty of customers for black baldie calves. Just this morning, I had a request for five hundred of them over the next two years."

Cady recalled the man he'd been meeting with when she and the boys arrived at his ranch that morning. "That's a lot," she said, impressed.

Jeb moved to sit beside her on the sofa. He settled his computer on his lap so she could see the screen, too. "I'll have to purchase at least two hundred and fifty cows or heifers and decide whether to invest in a couple of bulls or continue breeding the way I have been thus far, via artificial insemination."

Jeb went on, explaining the pros and cons of both, using different internet sites to further illustrate his points.

"Sounds like a big decision," Cady said, surprised by the depth of his knowledge and consideration.

He nodded. "It is. I could make more money in the long run from a bull, but the up-front cost is daunting, and there's no guarantee his genetics would be as good as what I could currently buy." Jeb glanced over at the picture on Cady's laptop. "And here I thought what I was doing was interesting," he drawled.

JEB WASN'T THE KIND of guy to feel jealous. But he definitely felt a twinge of something when he noted the dozen shirtless, jeans-and-hat-clad hunks currently appearing on Cady's computer screen.

She sighed. "It's an attachment, sent to me by my assistant, Marissa Adams. The advertising branch at Texas Star Marketing Group is pushing the marketing division to make a recommendation on the spokesmodel for the Hanover Horseshoe account, sooner rather than later, and everyone wanted my opinion."

Happy their old camaraderie was returning, Jeb teased, "And what is your opinion—having seen all the guys give their best come-to-bed-with-me looks?"

She grinned at his droll assessment and shook her head in exasperation. "First of all, sex always sells and you know it. And so do the models and their booking agents, hence the tone of the portfolio photos."

Which was, even Jeb had to admit, pretty darn sexy.

She clasped her hands together and lifted her arms

above her head, stretching languidly. "Second, I don't have an opinion, at the moment." Having apparently worked the kinks out, she dropped her hands back to her lap and continued. "We're going to have to talk to them. Find out who can memorize a script and be disciplined enough to sit for the photos for the print campaign, as well as be reliable enough to travel around to the trade shows, and county and state fairs, for however long this campaign runs."

Jeb studied her delicate profile. "Sounds grueling."

Her soft lips pressed together. "It will be. But that's not my biggest worry right now."

Cady signed out of the email function, shut the lid to her computer and leaned forward to set the laptop on the coffee table. As she did so, the hem of her khaki shorts rode up, giving him a nice view of her sleek, lissome thighs.

Jeb shifted his glance, only to encounter her curvaceous calves and slender ankles. She had slid off her flip-flops when she sat down, and her bare feet and pink toenails were feminine and pretty.

Wishing he could give in to his desire, haul her onto his lap and kiss her again, Jeb recalled his promise not to put the moves on her again tonight, and asked instead, "What is your biggest worry right now, then?" And why, he wondered with concern, did she suddenly look so stressed?

Obviously, oblivious to the nature of his thoughts, she lay her head back on the sofa and closed her eyes, her hair fanned out like a silk halo. She drew a deep breath, her breasts pushing against the cotton of her T-shirt, then rubbed the bridge of her nose, opened her eyes and turned her head to face him. "I have to decide whether or not to let my bosses know that I may soon be requesting a work-mostly-at-home schedule in lieu of an actual maternity leave."

Jeb put his computer aside, too, and turned toward her. His knee nudged her thigh, so he adjusted his leg so they were no longer touching. "You think it will be a problem?" He wished he didn't know how soft her lips were.

"No. They know I've been trying to adopt for several years now. And they've said it won't be an issue if I want to keep working and bringing in income instead of taking unpaid time off." She sighed. "I've been there long enough. They know what I can do and will work with me."

Jeb imagined that was so. Cady was one extraordinarily capable businesswoman. "Then…?"

She rubbed at an imaginary spot on her shorts. As an afterthought, tugged the hem down toward her knees. "I've come so close, several times, and dutifully informed the human resources department at work, only to see it all fall apart for some reason or another."

Jeb could see how that would be embarrassing as well as disappointing.

Cady swallowed, her anxiety evident. "I know I should go ahead and talk to them again, but I'm afraid doing so will jinx the adoption, and that I won't get the baby, after all."

He caught her hand in his and tightened his grasp. "Nothing bad is going to happen."

She bit her lip. "These situations are always fraught with peril, even under the best of circumstances," she told him with a catch in her voice.

Jeb sent her a reassuring look, gave her hand another

squeeze and reluctantly let go. "If it's meant to be, it will happen, Cady." And if it wasn't, he was sure she would find another way to get what she wanted. In fact, he would see to it.

Cady shot him a glance from beneath her lashes. "You're full of clichés tonight," she murmured, not seeming to mind the intimate turn the conversation had taken.

He shrugged, aware he didn't object, either. "I don't know a lot about adopting babies. But I know this. Where there's a will, there's a way. And someday soon you're going to be one fantastic mother."

CADY WENT TO SLEEP shortly thereafter, Jeb's encouragement still ringing in her ears.

She woke to the sound of her cell phone and the sight of sunlight streaming into the guest room. Groaning, she grabbed the telephone and put it to her ear.

"Hello," she whispered, hoping the boys hadn't been awakened by the chimes.

"Well, we're finally in Sydney!" Suki announced from the other end of the connection.

"Hey, Cady," Hermann chimed in.

She yawned and struggled to sit up. Hard to believe her sister and brother-in-law had been traveling all that time. "You must be exhausted."

"Very," Hermann confirmed. "Neither of us could sleep on the plane."

"How are the boys?" Suki inquired with maternal anxiety. "I miss them so much that I wish I could come home already!"

As if on cue, Dalton popped his head in Cady's room.

Finn followed. Then Micah. "Is that Momma?" Dalton asked.

"And Daddy," Cady confirmed with a grin. "Want to say hello?"

Bedlam followed as the three boys jumped on her bed. Cady switched on the speakerphone. Then everyone talked at once until, bored, Dalton jumped back off the bed. "Where's Our Friend Jeb?" he asked loudly.

"Yeah, I'm hungry," Finn stated, following his brother.

"I hungry, too," Micah added.

Without further ado, they dashed out.

"Did they say...Jeb—as in Jeb McCabe?" Suki asked in shock.

Cady cringed and switched off the speaker. She had been hoping to avoid that part of the story until Suki and Hermann returned home.

"Jeb is there...at this time of day?" her sister persisted, not bothering to mask the faint note of disapproval in her tone.

Hermann cleared his throat and said, "Honey, I'm going to see where our town car is."

Suki used her husband's absence to continue the third degree. "Cady, what is going on?" she demanded sternly.

Cady cringed, imagining the well-meant but misguided lecture sure to follow. "Jeb offered to help me out with the boys."

Her sister huffed. "Probably on the spur of the moment, unless I miss my guess."

Cady ran a hand through the tangles of her hair, then got up to find a brush. "What's wrong with that?" She climbed back into bed and began to brush her hair with her free hand.

"Cady, I know you've always had a secret thing for him…"

She rolled her eyes. "I have not!"

"Okay. Deny it if you must. But when it comes to anything but simple friendship, Jeb is a very bad bet. Just ask Avalynne Stone."

Jeb was right, Cady realized with sudden sympathy. The way he had once ditched his bride at the altar was still on everyone's mind, some ten years later.

"He has the attention span of a gnat," Suki continued.

Cady thought about his changes he had planned for his career, yet again, and tried not to sound defensive. "He likes to shake things up every once in a while. So what?"

"So," Suki retorted archly, "you are a planner."

Cady switched the phone to her other ear and resumed brushing tangles from her hair. "We're only talking about two weeks," she said heatedly.

A longer pause followed. "He's planning to stay with you and the boys for *two weeks*?"

Cady swore at her obvious misstep. The less her sister knew, the better. "If he wants to win his bet. It's a long story."

Hermann's voice mumbled in the background.

"Okay, okay," Suki said, sounding irritable. "Our car is here, honey. We have to go check into the hotel. I'll call you later."

She wished Suki wouldn't, but given that she was watching the boys, there was no way she could avoid it. "Talk to you then." Frowning, she hung up.

Jeb appeared in the doorway. He, too, looked as if he had just awakened. A golden-brown shadow rimmed his face, and his hair was tousled. He wore a pair of gray-and-white-striped cotton pajama pants, slung low on his hip, and a marine-blue T-shirt that brought out the sexy hue of his eyes.

"The boys wanted cold cereal and milk. Is that okay?" He came in for a closer look. "Are you okay?"

"Why wouldn't I be?" Flushing self-consciously, Cady jumped out of bed. They had turned the thermostat down before going to sleep, and it had gotten chilly overnight. Acutely aware of the way her lace-edged camisole pajama top was clinging to her breasts, Cady struggled into a matching pink cotton cardigan.

"I don't know." Jeb watched her rummage around for her flip-flops, one of which had gotten shoved under the bed. "You sounded upset just now, on the phone."

Cady stood and slid her feet into her sandals. "You know Suki," she muttered bad-temperedly. "No one is ever good enough for me."

"Meaning me," Jeb supposed. "Or someone else?"

Cady winced, realizing that, in her highly emotional state, she had just blurted out way too much. "Meaning...my sister wants me to have something amazing like what she and Hermann have found together. But the odds are stacked against me, since I am not currently dating anyone and haven't been for a while. And for the record," Cady added in a rush before Jeb could interrupt, "I did not intimate to Suki that you and I are or will ever be anything more than friends."

A corner of his mouth lifted in a speculative grin. "Meaning you didn't tell her we kissed," he drawled in a low, sexy tone that had her wishing he would throw caution to the wind and take her in his arms all over again.

"Kissing!" Three young voices shouted in unison as her nephews stumbled into the room. Gagging noises followed. "Blech! Yecchh! Gross!"

Cady propped her hands on her hips. Now Suki would know and have to weigh in on this, too. Unless, Cady thought quickly, she could make the boys forget what they had accidentally overheard. "Did you boys all finish your cereal?"

"Yeah, and we're still hungry." Dalton scowled.

"Can we have cookies?" Finn asked.

Jeb smothered a laugh.

Cady mimed her astonishment. "Cookies!"

The boys exchanged glances. "Momma lets us have them," Dalton declared audaciously.

Cady knew that was true. Later in the day, anyway. Figuring she would prefer to have her dietary indiscretion revealed the next time the boys talked to their mom, rather than her momentary lapse where Jeb was concerned, she nodded. "One each. And then we're getting dressed and going into town to accomplish the first thing on Momma's to-do list."

Dalton stood up straighter while Finn bounced on her bed. "What's that?"

Cady caught Finn before he could bounce off into the nightstand. She lifted him in her arms. "Get haircuts."

Jeb reached down and plucked Dalton and Micah, who were both begging to be picked up, too, into his arms. He held them against his chest. "Does that have to be this morning?" he asked.

Unable to see what the problem was, Cady nodded. "Suki made three simultaneous appointments for them at the salon, for nine-thirty." She rubbed Finn's back while he rested his head on her shoulder. Keeping her eyes meshed with Jeb's, she asked, "Do you have something scheduled?"

"I was supposed to talk to an insurance agent in town at nine-thirty, about the cost of insuring a bull, should I want to go that route. I was hoping we could all go together, and that can still happen if I reschedule."

Cady caught his arm before he could head for his phone. "There's no need for that. You can drop us at the salon and go on your way...."

Jeb glanced at her fingers, which were curled around his biceps. With his blue-gray eyes crinkling at the corners, he drawled in a low, sexy voice, "You wouldn't be trying to make me lose the bet, now, would you? By encouraging me to part company and be disqualified?"

Abruptly aware she had held on far too long, Cady let go of his arm. "Not a chance." Still savoring the feel of his warm solid muscles, she stepped back and continued cheerfully, "I'm as curious as you are to find out if you can go the distance."

And more importantly still, if I can keep my distance from you!

Chapter Five

Jeb parked in front of the Main Street Salon, slid out of the SUV and swiftly circled around to help Cady out of the passenger seat.

Clasping her elbow, he steadied her as her sandals hit the sidewalk. "You sure you can handle this?" he said quietly, inclining his head at all three boys, who were still safely strapped into their booster seats.

"Positive," Cady said.

He remained skeptical.

"Seriously, they have calmed down so much in the last twenty-four hours! Plus I think it really helped them to talk to their mom and dad this morning on the phone. To know that even though Suki and Hermann aren't here physically, they are still only a phone call away."

"As am I. So," Jeb said. "If you need me, just call, and I'll cut the meeting with Greg Savitz short. Otherwise, I'll meet you at the park across the street in an hour. Or sooner, if the session wraps up more quickly than anticipated."

Together, Cady and Jeb got the kids safely out of the car and into the salon. The three stylists were waiting. Jeb smiled and his wide shoulders relaxed. "I'll see you in a while. Boys, be good for your aunt Cady."

"Where is Jeb going?" Dalton asked unhappily as he climbed onto the swivel chair designated for him.

Finn stopped just short of his seat and twisted around to look in the direction Jeb had disappeared. The four-year-old's lower lip slid out into a pout. "Yeah. How come he's leaving us?"

"He has to see an insurance agent. He'll be back in a little bit," Cady said, realizing too late she and Jeb should have gone over with the boys what the plan was for the morning, before he departed.

Cady took Micah to the stylist who was waiting for him.

As soon as he saw the cartoon-decorated plastic cape and the booster seat in the salon chair, he shook his head and grabbed on to Cady for dear life. "Noooo!" he wailed in sudden panic. "Don't want haircut…"

Cady plucked him off the floor and held him in her arms. "Honey, it's all right, I'm going to be right here." She patted him soothingly on the back. "This is Sally, and she is just going to cut your hair."

"Noooo!" Micah screamed hysterically, wreathing his arms in a noose around Cady's neck.

Finn and Dalton looked over in alarm. Simultaneously, they attempted to pull off their capes. "If he's not doing it, I'm not doing it!" Dalton eluded the reassuring touch of the stylist and scrambled down from his chair.

"Me, neither!" Finn shouted in solidarity.

It was all Cady could do to hold Micah, never mind make a grab for his brothers. "Boys!" she shouted as they dashed for the exit.

And that was when two people Cady really did not want to see walked in.

Looking as incredibly gorgeous as ever, with her deep tan, wildly curling auburn hair and slim, toned body, Avalynne Stone came toward Cady with outstretched arms.

The squirming Micah in her grasp made a hug hello impossible. Which was just as well, Cady thought. Had she hugged Jeb's ex-fiancée hello, propriety would have required that she also hug Avalynne's mother, Dorothy—who was standing there, as dour and disapproving as ever.

Cady held on to the now silent but still furiously wiggling Micah. "Hello, Avalynne."

The young woman smiled. "Cady."

Dorothy Stone merely nodded.

In the meantime, the salon receptionist made it to the door before the two older boys could dart past the group of adults and escape. Sally joined her and stood in front of it, arms outstretched, blocking the way. The other two hairdressers came to claim their errant young customers, who only dug in their heels all the deeper.

Cady adapted the demeanor her sister used on such occasions. "Finn and Dalton, please stop misbehaving this instant and get back up in those chairs," she ordered sternly.

The boys refused to budge. "No way," Dalton said rebelliously, taking the lead.

"Not unless Jeb comes back and gets his hair cut, too!" Finn declared loudly.

To emphasize their rebellion, the two boys slumped on waiting area chairs and started kicking the magazine table.

Cady reached out a hand to try and stop them, but could do little without putting Micah down.

Sensing victory, Finn and Dalton glared at her and kicked so hard the magazines went flying.

Cady gasped at the mess.

At the continuation of the mutiny, Micah buried his head in her shoulder and resumed wailing with ear-splitting authority. "I. Want. My. Mommy!"

The Stones backed up with a mixture of dismay and disapproval.

The receptionist looked horrified. She sent a look at Cady that said, *Can't you please get those children under control?* Then slipped back behind the appointment desk at the front of the salon. "Can I help you?" She had to shout above the din.

Avalynne put both hands over her ears and shouted back, "Mother and I were going to see if we could get walk-in appointments this morning."

"Obviously," Dorothy said stiffly, looking irked by Finn and Dalton's truculent behavior and Micah's sobbing, "this is not a good time. We'll make appointments and come back. When it's quieter."

"It'll have to be soon, though," Avalynne said, leaning over the check-in counter to be heard. "I'm only going to be in town a few days."

And then once again, the door opened, the customer bell sounded…and Jeb McCabe walked in.

Silence fell in the salon.

Finn and Dalton immediately stopped kicking and sat up in their chairs, and Micah, taking his cue from his older brothers, stopped crying as abruptly as he had started.

And this time, Cady noted, there was no stopping Avalynne. She closed the distance between them and gave Jeb a warm lingering hug. Her mother, on the other hand, looked at him much as she had the day he had left her only daughter at the altar. As if she wanted to punch him in the face.

"Well, hi, stranger," Avalynne purred.

Jeb hugged Avalynne cordially and then drew back.

"We should get together," she said meaningfully, looking deep into his eyes.

"You're only in Laramie for a short while," Dorothy reminded her.

Avalynne ignored her mother's disapproval with the same deliberation she always employed. "I always have time to see Jeb, Mom. So…" She smiled again in a way that said she had eyes only for the sexy cowboy in front of her. "Call me, will you, stranger?"

His expression congenial but otherwise inscrutable, Jeb nodded.

Avalynne and Dorothy finished making their appointments for later that day and walked out.

Jeb turned to the boys. He surveyed them with an inquiring look that spoke volumes about his disapproval. "What's going on here, fellas?"

Micah launched himself out of Cady's arms and into Jeb's.

"We don't want to get our hair cut," Finn and Dalton explained in unison.

"I don't think you guys have a choice," Jeb said, speaking to them with the respect he would have given an adult. "Your mom made those appointments. She asked Aunt Cady to bring you here today, in her place. Your mom is going to expect you to follow through."

Finn and Dalton sighed. "All right."

"But before you do that, you need to pick up all

these magazines and put them neatly on the table. And apologize to the ladies in the salon for making such a ruckus."

"Okay." Sighing, the boys did as commanded, while Cady looked on with a feeling of ineptitude and embarrassment.

Finished, Finn and Dalton climbed back up into the barber chairs they had bolted from.

Micah hid his face in Jeb's neck.

Jeb looked at Cady. She shrugged, not having a clue.

"He usually sits on Suki's lap," the stylist explained.

Jeb patted Micah's back. "You want to do that, fella? Sit on Aunt Cady's lap?"

"No!" the little boy said, rearing back to look into Jeb's eyes. "I want to sit on yours!"

Everyone turned to Cady to see what she thought.

Masking her hurt, she lifted her hands in surrender, not about to argue. Anything, she mused fervently, to end this humiliation. Even if it meant handing the bulk of the substitute parenting over to Jeb.

"SO WHAT NEXT?" Jeb said, as they walked out of the Main Street Salon.

Finn held on to the left side of Jeb's belt, Dalton the right. Micah was nestled in his arms. All looked cute as could be with their new, neatly layered hairstyles.

Cady walked beside them, trying not to feel discouraged that her three nephews so clearly preferred Jeb to her.

At ten-thirty, the temperature was in the low eighties. The sun was shining overhead in a cloudless blue sky.

It was a perfect June morning and the boys were still full of unspent energy.

"How about the playground on the other side of the town square?" she suggested finally. "It's not too hot yet. They could run off a little steam."

"Yeah!" the boys cried in unison.

Jeb nodded. "Sounds good to me."

Carefully, they walked to the corner, waited for the light to change and then crossed the street. Five minutes later, all three boys were climbing on the massive wooden pirate ship and fort in the playground.

Jeb purchased cold drinks from a vending machine and he and Cady hung out under a tree, watching the boys play.

"So what happened to your meeting with the insurance agent?" Cady asked, knowing it couldn't have been completed that quickly.

Jeb's sexy grin widened and laugh lines appeared at the corners of his eyes. "I rescheduled for nine o'clock this evening."

Cady didn't know whether to be grateful or annoyed that he had so little faith in her ability to manage the children, although his lack of faith *had* turned out to be warranted....

She frowned, pushing back the unwanted emotion welling up inside her. "That's awfully late."

He kept his eyes locked with hers. "Greg Savitz was okay with it. I told him I wanted to make sure the boys were asleep first."

She stiffened her spine and glared at him. "He knows you're helping me out?"

Jeb stretched his long legs in front of him and rested an arm on the picnic table behind her. "It's not as if it's a secret." He leaned close enough for her to inhale the brisk masculine fragrance of his aftershave. "Is it?"

Should it be? Cady wondered. She ignored the comforting warmth of his body so close to hers and stretched her legs out, too. "You are taking this bet seriously." She curled her toes in her sandals, flexed her feet.

Jeb followed the restive movements, then returned his glance to hers. Mischief and suppressed desire glimmered in his eyes. "Did you think I wouldn't?"

Wasn't that a loaded question, Cady thought drily to herself. If the contemplative looks he had been giving her all morning were any indication, he wanted to triumph in their wager, as well as follow his more primitive instincts and get her into bed. And that they could not have. Not and maintain their age-old friendship, anyway.

"Well..." She drew a deep breath and attempted to get the conversation back on a more sober track. "Thanks for coming back to help out with the haircuts."

He accepted her gratitude with a nod.

The kids popped up at the top of the pirate ship. Heads barely visible above the wooden side, they lifted their arms in energetic waves.

Jeb and Cady smiled and waved back, offering dual admonishments to be careful. The kids nodded in understanding and took off again.

Jeb's mouth crooked up as he watched the three boys go down the slide, one after another. "I figured getting their hair cut was going to be difficult."

Cady did a double take. "Why?"

Jeb shrugged. "Friends who have kids have talked about how some children are traumatized beyond belief by the barber's chair, so I assumed the worst."

Cady scowled in renewed embarrassment. "Suki never said anything about it being such an ordeal. I mean, I don't think they ever give her any trouble." *Not the kind they give me, anyway.*

Which in turn made her wonder what kind of mother she was going to be. The kind who just naturally did everything right, like Suki, or the kind who struggled with literally everything? And if that was the case, how was she going to manage completely on her own?

Jeb cupped her shoulders and gave them a companionable squeeze. "Come on now. Of course they give your sister plenty of grief, too."

Finally beginning to see why others might have such a problem with her adopting as a single mom, Cady replied, "No, they don't. She and Hermann are real pros at handling the kids. Just like you."

"Suki and Hermann have had a lot of practice parenting. Five years, to be exact."

Okay, so that was true. "And what's your excuse?" she quipped, knowing full well that Jeb had never come close to that level of commitment to anything except remaining a footloose bachelor.

He shrugged offhandedly. "I'm a McCabe."

Of course. Cady sighed in mounting frustration and averted her glance. "So you're just naturally good at taking care of children," she murmured. *Like everyone else in his family.*

He tucked a hand beneath her chin and guided her face back to his. "I'm not naturally good at anything, Cady," he told her pensively. "I have to work at everything."

The compassion in his eyes made it easy to confide,

"You'd never know it by the way you are around the boys." Her throat was thick with emotion.

Jeb brushed his thumb across her cheek, then dropped his hand. "I'm at ease because I've been around kids of all ages as long as I can remember." His deep voice sent another thrill coursing through her. "When I was growing up, I had to watch over and entertain my younger brothers and sister, and all four of us had to mind our cousins whenever the extended family got together, which was pretty often. So I just learned. By doing. Just as you will." He reached over and gave her hand another reassuring squeeze. "I mean, wasn't that the plan of this two-week babysitting gig to begin with?"

How was it, Cady wondered, that Jeb always made her feel better? Feel as if she didn't have to live in anyone's shadow?

"Cady!" Finn shouted from the very top of the pirate ship.

Dalton joined him.

Down below, Micah was sitting in the sand around the base of the ship completely oblivious to everything as he concentrated on pushing the sand around with a stick and a rock.

And then everything changed, as two more cars pulled up in the lot. Doors opened and half a dozen pretty little girls, ranging in age from three to eight, piled out.

JEB WOULDN'T HAVE believed it if he hadn't seen it.

The jaws of all three boys dropped in awe as the giggling, shouting girls raced toward the ship, their moms following. For a long second, Cady's three nephews simply stared, as if they'd been hit by Cupid's arrow.

Trying not to notice how right it felt to be sitting here on the picnic table bench like this, with his arm around Cady's shoulders, Jeb leaned over to whisper in her ear. "I think they're in love." He chuckled, wishing attraction and affection were as simple for adults as for kids. Because if they were…if nothing else stood in the way…he and Cady would have been an item a long time ago.

Bemused, she was watching the interplay. "The boys are, anyway. I don't think the girls are quite as smitten."

"That's because girls are much choosier when it comes to guys—at least at that age."

Cady wrinkled her nose. "Seriously?"

Jeb liked the idea of her leaning on him, even if it was just for information. He shrugged. "When you're five, a pretty girl is a pretty girl. I don't think there's a lot of distinction."

She crossed her legs at the knee and ran a hand down her calf. "How about at your age?"

Jeb watched the restless swing of her foot beneath the shapely curve of her leg. "A pretty girl is just a pretty girl." And Cady, in his view, reigned supreme among those.

He paused, taking in the dissenting twist of her lips. Suddenly, it was all he could do not to pull her over onto his lap and kiss her.

Still studying her, he inclined his head. "You don't believe me."

She stood and shoved her hands in the pockets of her trim, knee-length shorts. "I didn't say that."

Jeb tore his gaze from the way the cotton fabric tightened across her derriere. He quaffed the rest of his soft drink and stood, too. "*Something* is on your mind."

Cady swung back around to watch the kids.

Finn tagged a little girl and raced off. His freckle-faced quarry followed, dashing over the wooden ramps of the play-fort until she caught up with him and tagged him back. He wailed in excitement, then tagged her again, and on and on they went.

Cady crossed her arms beneath the soft curves of her breasts and nodded at the action. "It's interesting how, with a dozen kids over there, Finn only has eyes for that one pretty little girl, and she only has eyes for him." Cady swallowed and continued drolly, "They just keep going back and forth. He chases and catches her, they split up, then she chases him—"

Abruptly, Jeb had an idea where this was leading. "Are we talking about the kids now?" he interrupted, shifting so Cady had no choice but to look at him. "Or me and Avalynne Stone?"

Cady flushed. *Guilty as charged.* She ran a hand through her hair, pushing the thick strands off her face. "What makes you think...?"

Jeb lounged against one of the pillars supporting the open-air picnic shelter, and tilted his head toward her. "I saw the look on your face when I talked to Avalynne in the Main Street Salon."

Cady ran the sole of her sandal across the cement floor, but kept her gaze on him. "It's pretty clear Avalynne still has...if not exactly 'the hots'...then some feelings for you."

Once again, Jeb thought, Cady had his number.

He frowned, torn about what he wished he could confide but had promised not to reveal.

"It's not what you think," he said finally. "There is nothing going on between Avalynne and me, no romantic pursuit."

Cady went very still. "Then what is it?" she asked curiously.

"We're friends," Jeb stated honestly, as a fresh wave of guilt and resentment washed over him.

And, unluckily for him, coconspirators as well.

Cady looked at him as if she was aware he was holding something back. Then she sighed.

And just like that, the barbed wire fence went up around her heart again.

She adopted a brisk, businesslike demeanor. "Our bet won't be impacted by your personal life or professional obligations. Just as it won't stand in the way of anything that I have to do." She shrugged. "Wager or no, we still have to carry on with our lives and meet our respective responsibilities."

Which in turn made Jeb wonder. "Do you have appointments scheduled, too?"

"Actually—" Cady smiled "—I do have something set up for this afternoon."

Chapter Six

"Why are you looking at me like that?" Cady asked, keeping one eye on the boys. Finn was still playing chase with the pretty girl. Dalton was climbing to the lookout of the wooden ship. Micah was scooping sand.

"Like what?" Jeb asked, waving at Dalton when the little boy reached his perch.

"Like you think I'm making a mistake, commissioning a mural for the baby's room."

Jeb turned back to Cady. "It's not a mistake," he said carefully. "Plenty of parents do that for their babies."

"So…?" Cady pressed, sensing his skepticism.

He turned his pensive gaze on her. "I just figured you'd want to buy the clothes and diapers and crib first. Unless you're planning to borrow all that from your sister?"

Cady shook her head. "Except for a few keepsakes, and the baby things Micah is still using, it's all been donated to charity."

Jeb ran his palm across his jaw. "So you'll be starting from scratch."

She nodded, not sure why she suddenly needed Jeb's approval so badly, just knowing that she did. "Which is why I want to talk to the artist who painted Suki's boys' rooms." *I want to start making this reality instead of just a long-held dream....*

Jeb clamped a reassuring hand beneath her elbow. "Then we'll make sure it happens," he promised.

Soon after, they rounded up the boys and took them to the Daybreak Café for lunch. From there, they went to Jeb's ranch, and "helped" him care for his baby calves and mama cows. Cady captured a cute video on her cell phone, to send to Suki and Hermann, and then they all went home together.

Jeb took over supervising the boys while Cady prepared for her meeting with Gratia Hernandez. The fifty something artist was as warm and personable as Cady recalled.

"I'd love to do this for you," Gratia said, after the two of them had settled in the kitchen and gone over the particulars. "There are only two problems. First, I'm booked solid for the next three months, so the soonest I could get to your baby's mural would be the middle of September."

"I can live with that," Cady said. It would give her more time to figure out the design.

"And two, I don't travel outside of Laramie County anymore, so…"

"I have a solution for that as well." Cady poured them both some more iced tea. "I was thinking…since I probably won't be staying in my current loft for more than the first year…that I'd like to have the work done on a large canvas that I could take with me."

Gratia clapped her hands together. "That's a marvelous idea! Then, yes, I would love to do it for you."

The two talked a little longer about possible little girl motifs, and then Cady walked her to the door.

"I'm so happy for you," the artist said, engulfing her in a hug. "I didn't know you were adopting. Suki didn't tell me—"

Suki!

At the realization, it was all Cady could do not to groan out loud.

"Is there a problem?" Jeb asked, when she walked back inside.

Cady looked at all the boys, who were busy playing trains on the wooden track he had helped them set up in the family room. It was amazing how well-behaved they were when he was around.

She pressed the heel of her hand to her forehead and headed to the kitchen, with Jeb beside her. "I can't believe I forgot to tell Suki and Hermann, when I talked to them this morning, that I'm getting a baby."

Jeb's glance trailed over her lazily. "There was a lot going on."

She gathered up the iced tea glasses and spoons from her meeting with Gratia and carried them to the dishwasher. Suki would not have kept something like this from her, even accidentally.

A guilty flush started in Cady's chest and spread to her neck. "I didn't tell them at noon when I forwarded the call phone video from the park, either."

Jeb lounged against the counter and plucked a snickerdoodle cookie from the jar. He munched contentedly. "You've had a lot on your mind."

That wasn't it, either, Cady realized in mounting alarm.

He narrowed his eyes and downed more of his own iced tea. "You could text them now."

She certainly could. The only problem was…

She paused and bit her lip.

Jeb leaned closer still and asked ever so softly, "Is there some reason you don't *want* to tell them?"

FOR A SECOND, Jeb thought Cady wasn't going to answer him. She finished putting everything in the dishwasher, then grabbed the watering can and filled it with tap water.

She walked over to the window and began methodically watering the potted plants.

In a low voice, she confessed, "Hermann hasn't weighed in on the subject—and he wouldn't. He's always thought I should live my own life, my own way. But Suki thinks I'm making a mistake."

Jeb could guess how much that hurt. Cady adored her older sister and wanted her approval more than anything.

He inhaled the fragrant scents of mint, basil, oregano and sage. "Because you're not married?"

"Because she thinks—as always—that I'm foolishly limiting my options and selling myself short. That if I just wait awhile, I'll find the perfect man to marry, and have kids the old-fashioned way, just like she did. And you and I both know that's just not going to happen for me."

This was the old Cady—the wallflower—talking. Jeb hadn't seen this part of her emerge in a while. He didn't like it.

He studied the sober lines of her mouth. "Is that why you're adopting?" He edged closer, speaking just as quietly. "Because you've given up on finding anyone who would love you?"

Cady set down the empty watering can. They were

standing beneath the air-conditioning vent, and a sudden blast of air had her clamping her arms in front of her, warding off the chill. "Why did you think I was doing it this way?"

Jeb turned his glance away from the sudden tautening of her nipples beneath her blouse. He adjusted his posture to ease the pressure against the front of his jeans. "I don't know." He shrugged and concentrated on the darkening hue of her beautiful brown eyes. "I guess I just figured that you preferred to go solo, sort of the way I do—only you wanted kids and didn't want to be pregnant."

Turbulent emotion tautened her pretty features. "I would love to be pregnant," she admitted.

He watched her, unsure how to help. "Then?"

Cady made a face. "The idea of a strange donor... It has such an ick factor for me. I can't do it."

Jeb had to admit he didn't like the idea, either. And how weird was that? It shouldn't matter—and he shouldn't be thinking about it, either.

"Plus, I've got only one ovary..."

He blinked, certain he hadn't heard right.

She let out a shaky breath, met his eyes and reluctantly explained, "I had surgery a few years ago on an ovarian cyst that got infected. They had to remove it and the fallopian tube on that side. Which leaves me with only a fifty percent chance of getting pregnant, under the best of circumstances."

Cady had been in the hospital? She'd had surgery and he hadn't known anything about it? He looked at her in shock. "You didn't tell me that."

She lifted a hand with a mixture of apology and regret. "Because I knew if I had you would have come to Houston. Truth was, I really didn't want you to see me then, because I was a hormonal wreck and I looked and felt terrible. Besides, Suki and Hermann were there."

Jeb put his hands on her shoulders and held her there when she would have run away from what was happening between them. "I wouldn't have cared if you were a mess, emotionally or physically."

"I know." She sighed and made no move to extricate herself from his protective grip. "That's what made it so hard." Her mouth curved ruefully as she conceded in a low, trembling tone, "The fact that you would have been so understanding. If I'd looked at you then..." Her voice caught as she started to get choked up. She blinked rapidly, reining in her tears, and continued determinedly, "I probably would have..."

He let his hands fall to her waist and brought her even closer. "What?"

Cady's lips parted.

Jeb had the strangest sensation she wanted to say something to him that she considered forbidden, and then at the last minute, couldn't find the words.

Or maybe just wouldn't, he realized in frustration.

Swallowing, she edged away and continued, "I would have cried on your shoulder. And I didn't want anything that sad entering into our friendship. I didn't want us to become closer because of something like that, because a lot of times—from what I've seen—that kind of illness-induced intimacy just doesn't last, and it leaves the two people involved feeling awkward."

Jeb wouldn't have wanted Cady's embarrassment to come between them, either.

And the truth was, if he had seen her falling apart, he would have wanted to rescue her.

Later, she might have resented him for it.

Or just been mortified, and hence, angry about that.

"I understand," he said gently.

He still wished he could have rescued her from that and any other kind of pain. It didn't matter whether his gallantry was misplaced or not.

All he knew for certain was that his desire to protect Cady went a lot further than simple friendship.

"SO THERE YOU HAVE IT," Greg Savitz said, hours later, as he concluded his presentation.

"Thanks for taking the time to break it down for me," Jeb said to the agricultural insurance agent.

"You'll let me know what you decide to do?"

Jeb nodded. "It should be sometime in the next seven to ten days." They shook hands, left the office, then stopped when they saw who was waiting outside.

Avalynne was standing next to Jeb's pickup truck. Dressed for an evening out, in a short skirt, sequined top and heels, she was clearly expecting him.

Aware that anyone who drove past the corner of Main and Oak could see them, he hurried over. "About time you wrapped that up," she teased.

The thing Jeb had always liked best about his ex was her independence. The trait he'd liked least was her need to always be the center of attention. "How'd you know I was here?"

Avalynne tossed her head. "I was on my way home after dinner with the gals, and I saw your truck. I figured this was as good a time as any for us to arrange for a time to make the transfer."

They had been doing this for years. Why then was Jeb suddenly so uncomfortable about what was a simple transaction conducted in secret? "Can't you just put it in the mail?"

Avalynne scoffed. "Seriously?"

She had a point. That probably wasn't the wisest option. "Okay, then. I'll put a key under the welcome mat and you can leave it at my ranch house."

"I'm not comfortable with that, either." Avalynne pouted. "I like handing it over in person. It gives me a sense of accomplishment."

Of all the times for her to be more difficult and demanding than usual, this was the worst. Jeb regarded his ex-fiancée evenly. "We're not kids anymore, Avalynne."

"How well I know that!" she exclaimed. "It's all my parents point out to me now when I visit. Why aren't I married? Why haven't I gotten over you?" She sighed, the depth of her frustration apparent. "And on and on."

Jeb was frustrated and tired of the cloak and dagger aspect to their relationship these days, too. He thought about Cady and how she would take all this.

He exhaled and suggested matter-of-factly, "Maybe we should call it a day. Let it be over, once and for all."

Avalynne adopted a defiant stance. "I owe you. I'm not going to go on owing you."

A car slowed as it passed. Jeb sighed when he saw who was behind the wheel—one of Avalynne's mother's best friends.

He waved, demonstrating he had nothing to be ashamed of, even if—in the eyes of some—any conversation he had with his former fiancée would be scandalous.

When the woman frowned and drove on, he turned back to Avalynne. "I understand your resolve. If I were in your place, I would probably feel the same way. But doing it like this still makes me uncomfortable."

Avalynne shrugged and got out her BlackBerry, checking for messages. "There's no other way to do it, since my dad still does my taxes."

"You could ask him not to."

Avalynne rolled her eyes. "You know how complicated my returns are, since I have all that foreign money coming in, on top of whatever I make in the States from the sale of my paintings. Besides, how would I explain *not* using his CPA firm, when they do it for me practically for free? There would be *questions*, Jeb. It would embarrass him in front of his partners. And haven't we done that enough?"

Yes, they had.

As much as Jeb wished he could have a do-over for that particular moment of his personal history, and handle the situation some other way, he knew he couldn't. He and Avalynne had made a deal on what would have been their wedding day, an agreement that continued to this day. It would be dishonorable of him to break his vow to her. And if there was one thing he was, as a man and a McCabe, it was honorable to his core.

"Okay," he relented finally. "But the transfer will have to be at my ranch, after nine at night."

"How about two days from now? That would give me enough time. Can you make it 10:00 p.m., at your ranch?"

Eager to get it over with, Jeb nodded. Their meeting set, he said good-night to Avalynne and returned to Cady and their temporary wards.

Her sister's elegant home was as quiet as it had been when he'd left. He followed the smell of something good to the kitchen and found Cady taking a muffin tray out of the oven.

She was wearing pink-and-white cotton pajama pants and a V-necked pink T-shirt. Her feet were bare, her toenails painted a sexy pink. Her hair had been swept loosely into a clip on the back of her head, with tendrils falling down around her neck and against her cheek.

The makeup she'd been wearing earlier was gone. Her freshly scrubbed face looked younger and more vulnerable, and he yearned to explore the silky texture of her skin and lips.

He knew how she kissed. If she made love even half as well as she baked...

Unfortunately, he reminded himself firmly, that was not why he was here.

Jeb turned his attention to the hot, golden muffins brimming with bits of fresh peach. "Those look delicious."

Cady slipped her hands out of the oven mitts. "Let's hope they measure up to Suki's." She put her sister's recipe away. "Otherwise, come breakfast, the boys are going to be very disappointed."

"Maybe I should taste one," Jeb teased, enjoying the sweet domestic scene. "Just to be sure."

Oblivious to the impact she had on him, she grinned at his offer and opened the fridge. "Maybe we *both* should." She batted her lashes at him mischievously. "Want butter or the cholesterol-lowering substitute?"

He smiled. "Let's live dangerously and go with the butter."

Cady reached up into the cupboard and got out two plates, the movement lifting her breasts against the fabric of her T-shirt. She turned to hand him one. "Your meeting with Greg Savitz go okay?"

Jeb thought about what it might be like to come home to Cady like this every night. Not just for the duration of their wager. He nodded. "Yeah, it went fine." It was running into Avalynne Stone that bothered him.

Not about to discuss that with Cady, he looked past her.

The kitchen table was covered with stuff. Jeb nodded at her cell phone, and the pages of notes scattered around her laptop computer. "What have you been up to?"

Cady brought a basket of muffins to the table, then went back to get silverware, napkins and the butter. "I've been answering work email, and researching murals for baby girls." She grimaced slightly. "And reassuring my sister that the boys are okay..." her voice lowered emotionally "...and that I do know what I'm doing."

There was only one thing that could cause that look in her eyes.

His heart filling with sympathy, Jeb got out the milk and two glasses. "You told her about adopting the baby?"

Cady's chin trembled as she pulled out a chair. "It was as I feared." Averting her glance, she admitted in a low, choked voice, "Suki thinks the adoption is a mistake."

Jeb caught Cady by the shoulders and forced her to look at him. "You don't need her approval."

Her eyes shimmered. "But I want it, Jeb. She's the only family I have, since Mom and Dad died."

Jeb knew the car accident that had claimed her parents had been brutally hard on both sisters, but Cady most of all. Suki had already had Hermann by then, but for the last ten years, Cady had been rudderless in a lot of ways. He suspected that loss was behind her desire to have a family, no matter what she had to do to get one.

He held the chair for her, then sat down kitty-corner to her. "What did you tell her?" As they settled in, their knees touched beneath the table. Jeb made no effort to pull away. Nor, to his delight, did Cady.

She shrugged, resting her knees against his. "I said that it was easy for her to tell me not to do it when she already had everything *she* could ever want. An adoring husband, three darling kids, a beautiful home and a career she can back to whenever she wants, because she's so darn talented."

Jeb could imagine how that went.

He picked up one of the steaming muffins, scorching his fingers slightly in the process. "What did she say then?"

"The usual." Having burned her fingers, too, Cady blew on the tips to cool them. "That I'm more beautiful and talented and wonderful than I have ever let myself admit."

She frowned, relating with no small amount of irony, "That I could have everything she has if I would just give it a try, instead of dumping boyfriends right and left, before going into the phase where I work so hard and so much I don't have any at all."

She lobbed off a big chunk of butter and slapped it onto her muffin. It melted quickly and slid down the sides.

"Furthermore…" Cady began to pick up steam, her cheeks a very becoming pink as she began to eat "…Suki doesn't understand why I never bring any of the guys I do occasionally date home to Laramie to meet her and the family." She dabbed her mouth with a napkin and sat back in her chair. Chin high, she glared at Jeb. "It's like she has amnesia about all the times I did bring a guy home and he immediately fell in love with her. And out of lust—or whatever it was—with me!"

Fury made Cady even prettier.

So pretty, in fact, that Jeb couldn't take his eyes off of her. Or stop wanting to say to hell with propriety and promises and a purely platonic friendship, and haul her into his arms again.

"I'm tired of playing second fiddle, Jeb!" Cady flattened her hands on the tabletop. "I'm tired of wishing things are going to get better for me, while knowing it's never really going to happen."

Vibrating with pent-up emotion, she pushed away from the table and vaulted out of her chair. Throwing her hands up in exasperation, she stalked off, her hips swaying provocatively beneath the pajama pants.

"Maybe I will never have anyone look at me the way Hermann looks at Suki! Maybe no guy will ever really desire me, but—"

This self-flagellation had to stop.

Jeb vaulted out of his chair, too. "Are you nuts?"

Cady stopped in her tracks.

He caught up with her, not sure whether to shake her or simply prove her unequivocally wrong. "Can you not see how guys look at you all the time, everywhere we go?"

Cady scoffed and backed away, not stopping until her

spine rested against the marble countertop. "The way you look at me, you mean?"

She folded her arms in front of her, the movement pushing up her breasts. "Like I'm perfect friend material?" she taunted, her eyes glittering resentfully. "The kind of girl you want to have a bet with, but never take to bed?"

Jeb edged closer, his own pulse racing. "You're wrong about that." He was attracted to her. Damn attracted.

Disbelief shimmered in her eyes. "Am I, now?" she taunted softly, a pulse working in her throat.

"Yes." He came even closer. Planted his hands on the counter on either side of her. Leaned in. Aware she wasn't the only one suddenly taking unprecedented risks here, he said firmly, "You are."

For a long, telling moment, Cady remained motionless, seeming not even to breathe. She definitely was not backing down.

"Really," she drawled finally, lifting her chin another notch.

Jeb nodded and leaned in a little more. "Really."

"Then prove it," Cady said.

Chapter Seven

Was she daring him to put the moves on her? Jeb studied the pique in her eyes. It certainly seemed as if she was. "All right," he murmured, wrapping his arms around her and pulling her close. "I will."

He heard her soft gasp of surprise as his head slanted over hers, and then his lips were on hers, their mouths fusing as one, their bodies pressing together. Heat flooded through him. Lower still, there was an insistent ache that spoke volumes about how much he wanted her.

Jeb hadn't meant to do anything but prove his point in the most irrefutable way possible. He hadn't expected her to melt against him and whimper low in the back of her throat. Open her mouth to the plundering pressure of his. Wreathe her arms about his neck, go up on tiptoe, and kiss him back in a passionate way that left them both spinning out of control.

But that was exactly what was happening, and damned if he wasn't happy as could be to have their desire for one another confirmed in such an amazing way.

Cady knew it was a mistake, daring Jeb to make a pass at her, just as it was a mistake to allow him to actually take her in his arms. She should be concentrating on what she needed, focusing on the adoption and the baby she had always wanted, instead of worrying about how he saw her. But she couldn't help it. There was something about his stubborn independence and the secret shame of the past that drew her inexorably.

And once his kiss came, it was just as dangerously exciting, just as masterful and uninhibited, as before. She reveled in the hard, insistent demand of his mouth on hers. She had never been kissed like this, with such fierce possessiveness. Had never felt such need welling up deep inside her. He was so warm and strong and male, and so kind and giving, too. So sexy. So deliberate and determined. Jeb was kissing her as if she was already his woman, he her man, and she knew if their embrace continued, she'd have to admit that everyone—especially Suki—was right, and that she did have a thing for Jeb. Always had, always would.

It was just a shame, Cady thought, that he didn't want the long-term commitment of marriage and family, because she needed both if she was ever to be really and truly happy.

With effort, she broke off the kiss and pushed Jeb away. She was breathing hard, tingling all over, and perversely longing for more. Much more.

He looked at her questioningly. And once again, she knew—for both their sakes—what she had to say.

Forcing herself to be realistic yet again, she reminded him, "We're friends, Jeb. Good ones. But I want more than just a physical relationship with someone. I need the kind of all-encompassing romantic love my sister has in her marriage." And they both knew he would never give her that.

Jeb went very still.

For a second, Cady thought she might have hurt his feelings with her frank assessment of their situation.

Jeb threaded his fingers through her hair, gently brushed his thumb across her cheek. "You're right," he retorted, with the legendary McCabe determination. He looked deep into her eyes and a devilish smile tugged at his lips. "It is too soon for us to be making a leap from friends to something more." He pulled her closer and pressed a tender kiss on her temple, before drawing back again. "We need time to be together and see one another in a different light."

Cady trembled, longing to throw caution to the wind and kiss him again. "Why?"

After all, what was the point, if their relationship wasn't going where she needed it to go?

He stroked her lower lip with one finger, then lowered his mouth to hers for one last kiss. The warmth and hardness of his body pressed against hers. "Because we won't know what we can have until we try, and my need for you is real and potent…and it's not going to fade."

CADY WENT TO BED, her emotions in turmoil and the thrill of Jeb's kiss firmly in her mind. She woke, two hours later to an anguished cry.

Realizing it was Micah sobbing, she bolted from the room and raced down the hall. He was standing in his bed. "Shhh, baby, it's all right." She rushed to scoop him into her arms.

The toddler struggled to be free. "I want my momma!" he wailed.

Jeb came in, too. Clad in a pair of boxers and a T-shirt, hair standing on end, he looked as if he had been as sound asleep as she. "It's all right, little fella," he soothed.

Micah turned away, crying all the harder. "Momma, Momma, Momma…"

Jeb slipped out and went across the hall. Quietly, he shut the doors to Finn's and Dalton's rooms, then came back.

Cady continued patting Micah on the back, soothing him as best she could. "He's not all the way awake," she said. Reaching into his bed, she extracted his monkey and yellow blankie. She put them in his grip and continued murmuring sweet words of consolation in his ear.

Finally, Micah shut his eyes and slumped against her shoulder, still restless, but no longer crying.

Cady continued walking him around the room, patting him on the back all the while, aware that this was the first time Micah had chosen her over Jeb.

"You got it?" Jeb whispered, his faith in her evident.

Confidence growing, she nodded. Maybe she wasn't foolish to think she could handle parenting as a single mom, after all. It was just going to take more experience. The kind she was getting now.

Grateful to have Jeb there with her anyway, she touched his arm in thanks. "Go on back to bed," she whispered, wanting him to get all the rest he could, too. As her hand lingered on the strong curve of his biceps, she recalled the heat of their earlier kisses, and the joy his embrace had brought her.

And wondered if he was right to think they just needed to give romance a try. In the meantime… "I can handle this," she promised, looking deep into his eyes.

And, as it turned out, she could.

It took half an hour more of rocking and cuddling and soft, nonsensical singing, but eventually she was able to get Micah to a deep, relaxed sleep.

Cady eased the two-year-old back into his bed, tucked his monkey beneath his arm and covered him with his yellow blankie. She stayed a while longer, just to make sure he was asleep, then went across the hall to reopen his brothers' doors.

Tiptoeing in, she saw that Finn and Dalton were still sound asleep. With a wave of love washing over her, she adjusted their covers. Resisting the urge to check on Jeb, too, she returned to her own room and slipped back into bed.

Thrilled by her success, she fell asleep, dreaming of the day when she would have her very own baby to cuddle and rock to sleep every night.

The next thing Cady knew, sunshine was streaming in through the blinds, and three young voices were hushing each other loudly.

"Hey, I get to wake her!" Dalton said.

"No. I do!" Finn argued.

"Muffins!" Micah shouted.

Cady struggled to open her eyes, and found herself looking into a trio of eager little faces.

"We brought you breakfast!" Dalton said, thrusting a glass of orange juice and a napkin at her.

Finn held out a container of yogurt and a spoon.

Micah had the peach muffin.

And Jeb was right behind them, with a steaming cup of coffee in one hand, a tray in the other.

"Thank you, guys!" Cady said, feeling both touched and grateful. No one had ever done this for her before.

Realizing it was nearly eight, she sat up, lifting the tangled hair from her face and combing it into place with her fingers. "I didn't mean to oversleep."

Jeb plumped the pillows behind her back and fitted the tray over her lap. "We guys thought you could use an extra hour or two of shut-eye."

The boys climbed onto her bed and deposited their offerings on the tray. Excitement shone in their cornflower-blue eyes. "That's the only muffin that's left," Dalton reported seriously. "Me and my brothers ate the rest of them. Jeb didn't even get *any*."

"Oh, dear," Cady said, laughing and shaking her head. "I guess that means I'll have to make some more."

"Can we go to the playground again today, Aunt Cady?" Finn sat cross-legged to her right, while Dalton settled to her left. Jeb took up position at the foot of the bed. "Our Friend Jeb says it's okay with him if it's okay with you."

Cady looked into Jeb's sexy, blue-gray eyes and found that was indeed the case. "That sounds like a great idea."

Micah said nothing, but situated himself on the pillow next to Cady and snuggled up against her. And in that instant, she knew for certain the joy a family of her own could bring—even if the one she had now was temporarily.

"So HOW DO YOU WANT to do this?" Cady asked an hour later. Like Jeb, she was showered and dressed and ready to take on the day. The boys were still in their pajamas, but that could be easily remedied.

Jeb grinned at her, looking happier than she had ever seen him. As if playing house with her and the kids really agreed with him. He sauntered closer and took her hand in his. "I need to do a few things at the Flying M before we head for town."

Glad to have something to focus on other than the hot kisses they had shared the night before, Cady looked down at their entwined hands. Much as she tried, she could not force herself to pull away, any more than she could corral her fast-growing desire for him.

She swallowed and looked up at him with the most matter-of-fact expression she could manage. "You want us all to go?" Which would be what she'd prefer. "Or would you rather head over to your ranch alone?"

He tilted his head to study her and came closer, his warm breath brushing her temple. "Solo would probably be faster."

Cady knew he was right about that. With effort, she tamped down her disappointment. It was probably better they each had some breathing room and got back to reality, she reminded herself.

She extricated her hand from the cozy warmth of his and flashed a smile she couldn't really begin to feel, "I'll have them ready to go by the time you get back."

He brushed the curtain of her hair aside and pressed a fleeting kiss on the nape of her neck. "See you in forty-five minutes." Jeb smiled again and sauntered out, whistling.

Still tingling from the brief, evocative contact, Cady went to find the kids.

They were in the family room, playing with the enormously complicated train set Jeb had assembled the afternoon before.

"How come we have to get dressed if we're not

leaving yet?" Dalton demanded, reluctant to relinquish his toy.

Cady set the wicker basket down and got out the first set of clean clothing. "Because I promised Jeb we would all be ready to go when he got back. And you have to be dressed in something other than pajamas to go to the park," she explained.

Finn's face lit mischievously. "You gotta catch me first!" he cried, dashing up the stairs.

To Cady's dismay, the youthful rebellion spread.

"Me, too!" Dalton declared. He sprinted after his brother, then promptly headed off in another direction when he reached the top of the stairs. Micah followed quickly.

Cady groaned, wondering where the sweet boys who had thoughtfully brought her breakfast in bed had disappeared to.

Worse, Jeb was barely out the door, and here they were again—with her feeling exasperated and inept, and the boys completely out of control.

Trying not to think about the fact that the kids never behaved this wildly around anyone but her, Cady drew a stabilizing breath and moved to restore order, knowing it was not going to be easy.

Suki's home had over seven thousand square feet of space, which meant it would be tough trying to catch the little imps.

But first things first.

Cady went up the stairs and into their rooms to try and locate them. Naturally, they were not in the most obvious place, and giggles and rapidly running footsteps sounded all around her. Trying not to be a complete spoilsport, she let them have their fun for a little while longer.

Then she went down to the living room and waited, in full view of the sweeping front staircase. "Okay, guys! The game is over! It's time to come out now!" she called.

There was more muffled giggling. "No!" Dalton shouted.

"No way!" Finn and Micah agreed.

The doorbell rang.

Exhaling again, even more wearily, Cady headed for the door, where a deliveryman waited.

By the time she had signed for the big silver box with the white bow, all three boys were standing beside her once again.

"What's in there?" they demanded in unison, curiosity having won out over the need to put her through her paces.

Cady looked at the tag. "It's a birthday present for me, from your mom and dad." Soon she would be thirty-four. And although she was no longer depressed about marking the passage of another year, she wasn't exactly in the mood to celebrate it, either.

"Open it!" Finn shouted.

"It's not my birthday yet," Cady said.

Dalton hopped up and down. "But we want to see what's inside."

"We'll find out on my birthday," she promised, putting the package aside. "In the meantime, you guys have to get dressed or you won't be ready to go to the park when Jeb gets back here," she told them soberly.

Their interest in the game they had been playing was waning anyway, and ten minutes later, Cady had them all ready to go. But there was still no sign of Jeb, and the boys quickly grew stir-crazy. Chaos ensued when Micah began racing around like a battery-driven toy stuck on high speed, and that managed to rile his older brothers up all over again.

In the midst of all the commotion, Cady's cell phone rang. Realizing it was the Stork Agency, and hence potentially important, Cady lifted a silencing hand and said, "Guys, can you go upstairs to the playroom for a minute and find something quiet to do? I really need to answer this."

"Okay," the boys said, and dashed off in unison.

She answered and discovered her baby's birth mother on the other end of the connection.

"Is everything okay?" Cady asked.

"Yes." Tina Matthews took a deep breath. "I just wanted to talk to you a minute about something, and you said I could call you anytime."

"Of course you can," Cady was quick to insert. Aware her knees had started to tremble, she sat down on the staircase. "What is it?"

"I've been thinking about my baby and I wanted to do something for her before I give her up. And so I was wondering…."

The teen stopped and drew in a bolstering breath. "Would it be okay if I named the baby before you adopted her? 'Cause I really like the name Zoe, and she sort of feels like a Zoe."

After another pause, Tina asked hesitantly, "Does that seem stupid to you?"

Cady had an idea how hard giving up her child was for Tina. Cady wanted to do anything she could to make it easier.

"No, honey, it doesn't," she replied gently. "In fact, I think it's a very loving gesture." She looked up as Jeb walked in the front door. "And a good way to say goodbye."

Jeb gave her a quizzical look, but remained silent.

"I knew you would understand," the pregnant teen said in obvious relief. "Well, listen, I have to go."

"Call me anytime," Cady repeated gently.

"I will." She hung up with a click.

Jeb sat down next to Cady on the stairs, his hip and shoulder brushing hers. He looked at her, a question in his smoky blue eyes. Briefly, Cady explained.

He exhaled sharply. "Her request doesn't bother you?"

"No. Of course not." Cady basked in the comforting warmth of his body next to hers. She turned toward him slightly, searching his face. "But it bothers you, doesn't it?"

"From my perspective, it's one of two things." He frowned, clearly unhappy. "Either Tina Matthews is not as at ease with her decision to give up her child as she supposes."

Don't say that, Cady thought. *Don't even think it!*

Without considering the consequences, she reached out and took Jeb's hand.

He held on tight and brushed the back of her knuckles. "Or she is preparing herself for the coming separation and already starting to say her goodbyes. In either case—" he paused to compress his lips "—I really admire you."

Cady basked in his candor and strength. She had always wanted Jeb to respect and believe in her, now more so than ever. "Why?"

He stood and drew her to her feet, wrapping an arm around her and smoothing her hair with the flat of his hand. "This is a precarious situation and you're still going all out to pursue what you really want."

She leaned against him with a sigh. At times like this, it was hard to believe he didn't want family as much as she did. "You can't see yourself doing the same thing?"

"Adopting on my own? No. Going after what I really want…" He lifted her hand to his lips and kissed the back of it. "That's something else again."

CADY WAS ON THE VERGE of asking Jeb what he meant by that when a rebel yell sounded upstairs. Then quickly intensified. "Uh-oh," she said, reluctantly recalling her directive to the boys to entertain themselves. "I better go see what's going on up there."

Jeb started up the staircase. "We'll both go."

To Cady's disgruntlement, it wasn't pretty.

The boys had bypassed their playroom in favor of their mother's studio.

Magic markers were scattered everywhere. Rainbow-colored streaks decorated the carpet, Suki's beautiful glass-and-chrome desk, her bleached wood drawing table, and the white leather chair behind her desk. Drawings that had been tacked up on a room-length bulletin board were now defaced with big, bright scribbles.

Cady stared at the mess. "Oh…no, no, no…" Her sister was going to be furious!

Jeb strode forward. He plucked the two older boys off the low bookcases they had been standing on while they colored on their mother's drawings.

"Okay, fellas, the party is over. Let's clean up this mess."

"And then," Cady added sternly, "all three of you are getting a time-out." For once the boys did not protest the discipline.

Cady knelt and put out her palm. Micah, realizing he had done wrong, although maybe not quite understanding how, relinquished the marker he was holding.

Cady found the cap, snapped it back on the marker and proceeded to pick up several more. When she finally stood, she looked down and saw the bright black lettering on every pen: *Permanent. Nontoxic.*

She swore silently to herself, then said to an equally dismayed Jeb, "Well, the good news is the markers are harmless. The bad news is it's probably not going to come out. Of anything." She sighed unhappily. If ever they had needed proof that she was not capable of handling kids on her own, this was it.

"AUNT CADY IS REALLY MAD at us, isn't she?" Dalton observed, after the initial cleanup was completed and time-outs served, and Cady had gone off to research what to do next.

Utilizing the same calm, stern demeanor his parents had used in similar situations, Jeb sat down with the three boys for a heart-to-heart. "She's very disappointed. She doesn't understand why you're behaving this way."

Finn and Dalton exchanged guilty looks.

So something was up, Jeb thought, aware he was onto something. "Maybe you could tell me why," he coaxed gently.

The boys remained silent.

So they weren't ready to talk.

Maybe later, Jeb thought. "But I have an idea how you boys can make it up to her."

Relief shone in their faces as he explained his plan. The boys agreed not to breathe a word of it, lest they spoil the surprise.

He had just finished when Cady walked back in. Her face was pale with misery. She strode closer, her slender body tense, and brought him up to speed. "I looked online. The manufacturer's website offered no clue. So I phoned them."

Jeb stood. "And?"

Cady swallowed. "They said since these are artist's pens, the ink isn't meant to come off anything. I'm welcome to try any of the normal remedies, but they don't guarantee anything will work."

Whoo boy, Jeb thought.

"They told me I should have been more careful." She ran a hand through her hair. "So I called the best professional carpet cleaning service in the area. They confirmed it was probably hopeless."

"They weren't willing to try?"

A flicker of pain flashed in Cady's eyes. She shook her head in defeat. "They felt I would be wasting my money and it would be irresponsible of them to try, knowing what the outcome was going to be."

"Are you going to tell our momma and daddy what we did?" Finn asked sheepishly.

Cady sighed. "I think I'll wait until they get home," she said as the two older boys exchanged wary—almost disappointed—looks.

Jeb agreed. No sense worrying Suki and Hermann. If they knew, they might jump to the same erroneous conclusion Cady had: that the three boys were more than she could handle alone....

Tears welled in Micah's big blue eyes. He went to Cady and lifted his arms, asking to be picked up. "I want my momma," he wailed, bursting into tears.

She swung him into her arms and hugged him close, much the same way she had the night before. "I know exactly how you feel, buddy." Her maternal gentleness on full display, she walked him back and forth and rubbed his back until his tears subsided.

Jeb met Cady's eyes, perfectly willing to let her call the shots. "So what next?"

She compressed her lips in determination. "It may not work, but there are several things I can try for removing stains."

He knew the sooner she got to it, the better her chance of success, so he offered what he thought would be the most help. "Want me to take the boys elsewhere?"

Cady looked at him gratefully. "If you wouldn't mind."

JEB AND THE THREE KIDS headed off. Realizing he couldn't do it alone, he enlisted his mother's help, and together, they worked on their surprise for Cady.

After lunch, his mom said, "I really think you ought to go and see how Cady is faring with the ink stains. I'll watch the kids for you."

Jeb had to admit she had a better handle on the three boys than either he or Cady had. But then, she'd had years of experience.

"You sure it's okay?"

His mother smiled. "I've got the day off from the restaurant, and I love having little ones around. It gives me hope," she teased, "that one day you'll change your mind about marriage and have a loving wife and brood of your own."

Jeb knew his mom was matchmaking. The funny thing was, he didn't mind. Since he had kissed Cady and felt her kiss him back, he had known the days of them being just friends had passed. Something more was brewing. The challenge would be convincing Cady to admit she felt it, too.

He walked into Suki and Hermann's house and followed the music blasting out of the sound system in Suki's studio.

Cady was sitting cross-legged on the floor in front of a particularly bold scarlet stain on the pale carpeting. Her shorts had ridden up on her inner thighs, revealing sleek, sexy skin. Her golden-brown hair was twisted up in a messy knot on her head, and the scoop-necked, aqua T-shirt nicely molded her torso. She looked beautiful and kissable and frustrated as all get-out, and Jeb couldn't say he blamed her. For a woman who thrived on success, and hated to look bad in front of her glamorous, accomplished older sister, this was one hell of a mess. In Suki's private domain, no less.

"Where are the kids?"

He hunkered down next to her so he could be heard above the pounding, lively beat of the music. He wanted to see more of the normal confidence on her pretty face, instead of the moue of misery and defeat. "With my mom." He glanced at the array of products and cloths around her, trying hard not to notice how the neckline of her T-shirt gaped slightly as she worked, revealing the womanly curves of her breasts. "How's it going?"

"Not good." Cady sighed, planting her hands behind her. She leaned back on her arms, stretching her shapely legs out in front. "I've tried every remedy I could find. Rubbing alcohol, hairspray, acetone fingernail polish remover, baking soda and water, and stain gels and sprays. As you can see—" she gestured helplessly, sitting forward once again "—nothing has really budged it." She shook her head in defeat. "I'm about as far from a miracle as I can get."

Jeb bent to examine what she'd done. Some of the stains looked unchanged. Some actually looked worse. "Have you spoken to the carpet store?"

Cady met his eyes. "They said if Suki has any remnants, they could cut out the stained parts and patch it, but it's at least a hundred dollars per patch, and there are dozens of stains, so it might be cheaper in the long run to just replace the entire carpet."

He winced. "Ouch."

"Yeah, I know." She started to stand and Jeb offered her a hand up. "What are you going to do?"

Cady plucked up the various bottles and set them in the cleaner caddy. Shoulders slumped, she headed for the door. "Wait for Suki to come home, I guess."

Jeb followed her down the back stairs.

"And feel like a failure in the meantime," she added.

Cady set the caddy on the shelf unit opposite the washer and dryer. The depth of her despair made her look even more vulnerable. "I promised Suki and Hermann I'd take good care of the kids. I forgot to say anything about their home." She lifted her eyes to Jeb's with a disparaging twist of her lips. "Maybe I should have, hmm?"

"And maybe, once again, you're being too hard on yourself." Determined to comfort her, he impulsively pulled her into his arms and lowered his mouth to hers.

Chapter Eight

Cady knew Jeb was kissing her for all the wrong reasons. She knew the last thing in the world either of them should be indulging in was a hookup, born out of chaos and mercy, but she couldn't help herself. She wanted Jeb. Had since the very first time he had kissed her. So what if theirs was a tryst that might not ever occur again? So what if she didn't do things like this? It felt right. *He* felt right. So hard and big and strong. So tender and caring and gentle.

With a moan, she closed her eyes and luxuriated in the feel of his hands in her hair. With a chuckle, he removed the clip and let the strands fall around her shoulders. His fingers sifted through the length of it; his thumbs stroked her cheeks, her chin.

And still they kissed and kissed. Cady wrapped her arms around his shoulders and held on tight. She pressed her breasts and thighs against the firm muscles of his chest and legs.

His hands drifted lower, to her hips. When he eased one beneath the hem of her T-shirt, her skin tingled. Cady moaned again as his palm smoothed over her skin, beneath her bra, pushing aside the cloth to cup the weight of her breast. Heat jolted through her, centering in her heart and spreading outward. Her knees buckled, but it didn't matter. Jeb supported her with one arm, and the other slipped low, beneath her hips. Cupping her buttocks, he held her against him, the unexpectedly erotic alignment sending electricity streaming through her. The full-on pressure of his manhood was incredibly thrilling.

For the first time, Cady knew how it felt to feel beautiful, inside and out. To feel wanted past reason, and to want, as desperately and fiercely, in return.

Passion like this had always been denied her. But it was here now, spilling into their embrace until her bare toes curled and the sensations flowed. A desperate ache swirled between her thighs and she sighed at the exquisite torture of his fingers moving over her breasts again.

And still he kissed her, until she was straining against him, aware that nothing had ever felt so exquisitely delicious as his mouth moving on hers, or his hand sliding lower, across the plane of her ribs to her navel.

A snap and a zip later, and her shorts were falling to her ankles. As his hand moved even lower, her body dissolved in a white-hot glow. And then he had her, there, and she was so overwhelmed, the desire so powerful and all encompassing, she couldn't stop. Didn't *want* to stop.

Cady let go of his shoulders and found his belt. The zipper to his fly. The leanness of his hips and the flatness of his lower abs. Lower still, the silky, pulsing heat.

Her hand closed around him.

His kisses grew more ferocious, his mouth absorbing the hungry, impatient sounds that rose in their throats.

Shifting again, he lifted her to the top of the dryer and pulled her to the edge.

Cady opened her eyes, saw him looking down at her, eyes smoldering, body taut.

For the first time in days, she didn't feel like a failure. Instead, she felt she was everything Jeb had ever desired.

She smoothed her hands across the handsome planes of his face. "I want you," she whispered.

He shifted her closer, the tension gathering. "I want you, too."

He opened her thighs, urging her forward, easing the way and possessing her with a subtle rhythm that had her body throbbing in every extremity.

Until there was no more holding back, no more careful friendship between them. It was all hot, long, out-of-control kisses and wet, sliding silk. All possession and need and want. Until finally the satisfaction came, and Cady slumped, spent and shaking, in the warm, protective circle of his arms.

THE LAST THING Jeb had meant to happen was this, but there was no denying the powerful force of their hot, passionate, adrenaline-fueled sex. Joy rose up inside him, followed by a masculine satisfaction that was soul-deep. "Damn, Cady," he whispered against the sweet, slender arch of her throat. "That was amazing."

She was silent, shell-shocked, still trying to catch her breath.

And he knew from the fleeting flicker of guilt in her eyes that as quickly as she had come into his arms, she would leave.

Unless he found a way to get past her dazed trepidation, to her heart.

He leaned back to survey her tenderly and give her the physical space she seemed to need. "But it could have been a lot more romantic." Still caging her loosely in his arms, he gently kissed her temple.

Cady splayed her hands across his chest, keeping him at bay. "It was fine."

Fine was never a good adjective for a woman to use in the midst of the afterglow.

But aware that the slow, tender courtship she deserved had been edged out by their skyrocketing desire, Jeb caught her wrist and lifted it to his lips.

"Let me take you to bed," he murmured, inhaling the feminine scent of her skin, enjoying the just-loved way she looked. "And do it right this time."

Cady released a shaky breath. She pushed him aside and jumped down off the dryer. While scrambling to pull on her clothes, she averted her glance and said, "That's not a good idea. Because that would imply this could become a regular thing between us," she finished stubbornly, pulling the zipper up and doing the snap. She pushed her bra back into place and tugged down the hem of her T-shirt before looking at him once again. "And it won't be."

Jeb took his cue from her and reassembled his own clothing. "Why not?" They were minutes away from making love like there was no tomorrow, and he could already feel her withdrawing emotionally.

Cady inhaled a jerky breath and shoved her hands through her hair, smoothing the messy strands. "Because we're not in love with each other, and we're headed down two very different paths." She found her clip and put her hair back up. "I'm about to become a mother, Jeb."

She certainly had the demeanor of one now. Responsible, no-nonsense, supreme defender of her turf...

Aware that she was scared by the intensity of what had just happened, but had no reason to be, he followed her out of the laundry room. "I know that."

Her spine ramrod straight, Cady headed for the dishwasher and began unloading it. "Your ranch is in Laramie, and I live over two hundred miles away from here."

Not about to let what they had just discovered go, Jeb moved in to give her a hand. "I know that, too," he stated quietly, stacking clean plates.

Cady swung around to face him. "It wouldn't work in the long haul."

Jeb wasn't so sure about that.

"And I'm not interested in the short term." She lifted a hand, cutting him off. "It was good...you know that. But a one-time occurrence was all it will ever be."

"WHAT'S WRONG?" Suki asked Cady, when she called to check in that evening, after the boys were in bed.

Cady pushed back from her laptop computer, temporarily putting her work email aside. "What do you mean?" she asked uneasily.

"You sound funny."

Cady felt funny. Her lovemaking with Jeb had been so far out of the realm of possibility, she still didn't know quite what to make of it.

The chemistry was there, of course. Wow, was it there! But nothing else about their lives meshed. And much as she wanted to, she couldn't ignore that, couldn't deviate from her long held plans for her future.

"I'm tired," Cady fibbed.

"I'm sure you are, but I also know you've got something else on your mind," Suki continued with sisterly intuition.

I'm afraid Jeb and I have permanently screwed up our friendship by making love.

"Like maybe your birthday tomorrow…"

Cady cringed at the reminder that she was nearly another year older. "I'm not upset about that." Not like I normally am, anyway. *Not when I have so many other things to wring my hands over.*

"You sure? Thirty-four is…"

Cady guessed where this was going. "Getting up there?"

"Cady. Come on." Suki was not entertained by her sister's droll remark. "You know what I meant!"

"I do." She forced herself to look at the bigger picture. "But I have a lot to be thankful for this year. A baby to adopt." *A man who made me feel like I'm beautiful and amazing…* Even if that sensation was fleeting, she would always treasure the memory of that wondrous moment.

"You, Hermann and the boys." Cady continued her gratitude list. "The present you had delivered today…"

"So if that's all good, then what is it?" Suki insisted, her low voice reverberating with concern. "And don't tell me nothing. I can sense it."

Cady knew she had to tell her sister something, or the inquisition would persist forever. So she revealed what she felt she could. "The boys got into the colored markers in your studio." Cady drew a deep breath. "They decorated damn near everything. I've tried every remedy possible, and it won't come out."

Suki was silent for a painfully long moment. Finally, she said, very calmly and gently, "Okay. Is everyone all right?"

"Yes," Cady admitted in relief. "The kids are aware they did something wrong and they are sorry. They helped pick up the pens, but the damage they did appears to be as permanent as the ink in the markers."

"Well," Suki sighed, "if that's all…"

Cady knew how precise her sister could be. How much she loved elegance. "We're talking some major damage, Suki. Plus, they decorated your sketches for the film."

"I've got copies of everything I've drawn to date—it's been scanned into my computer. As far as the rest…I've been wanting to redecorate in there, anyway. Paint again and put in a wood floor, maybe another kind of chair and drafting table." She sighed. "And with the money I'm making on this job, I'll have the funds—and now the incentive—to do it."

Cady blinked, wishing all the problems in her life could be solved that easily. "So you're not mad at me?" she asked carefully.

Suki laughed. "They get into stuff when I'm there, too, you know."

No, Cady hadn't. Her sister always behaved as if her life on the home front was absolute perfection.

"And they are probably a little ticked off at me for leaving them to go to Australia. It'll be fine. I'm just glad it's nothing worse."

Cady sagged in relief. Maybe she wasn't as inept

at this mothering stuff as she had feared. Maybe she didn't need someone like Jeb in her life, helping out, to be successful in the parenting department.

"Now…about your birthday celebration…" Suki continued in her usual, I'm-the-accomplished-older-sister-so-I get-to-take-charge manner.

"I'm fine waiting until after you get back from Australia. In fact, I would much prefer to celebrate it after I bring the baby home."

Cady suddenly had the feeling she wasn't alone. She turned to see Jeb standing in the kitchen doorway, looking as if he was upset about something. What, she couldn't fathom, since he'd already made it plain that birthdays were nothing he lost sleep over.

"Suki okay?" he asked after she finished her conversation and hung up the phone.

Noting that whatever concern he'd had seemed to have vanished, Cady explained Suki's reaction to the damage to her studio.

He nodded, apparently not surprised that she had taken the marker catastrophe in stride. "That's good. Listen, I've got to go over to my ranch for a while, to take care of a few things there, and then briefly stop by my mom's after that. You going to be okay here?"

Was that guilt on his face? Unease? Regret? All Cady knew for sure was that he wasn't being completely open with her about his plans for the evening.

But then maybe that was to be expected, she told herself. Maybe, after their impetuous lovemaking, he wanted to resurrect the boundaries between them, as surely as she did. And she could hardly blame him for that.

"YOU'RE LATE," Avalynne said, when Jeb emerged from his pickup truck.

He crossed to where she was sitting on his darkened front porch, a thick manila envelope in her lap.

"Sorry." He worked to mask the impatience in his voice. "It couldn't be avoided."

Avalynne handed him the package. "It's all there."

Jeb knew it was.

"You can check if you like."

He shook his head.

"Which means we only have to do this…what?" Avalynne rose. "Two more times?"

"I've been thinking about that." Jeb unlocked the front door to his ranch house and led the way inside. "Maybe we should just call it a day."

She vetoed that suggestion, stubborn as ever. "I told you. A promise is a promise."

He opened the wall safe and stuck the envelope inside. A couple of weeks ago he would have agreed. Now his attitude was different. There was too much at stake for any of this to be misconstrued. And if people knew… "It's time we moved on with our lives."

"Like you are now?" Avalynne watched him replace the painting in front of the safe.

When he didn't reply, she told him, "Everyone is talking about the bet you made with Cady Keilor. For the record, *no one* thinks it is all about the kids."

The last thing Jeb wanted from his ex was advice on his private life, well meant or no.

He turned around, ready to walk her out. "Then for the record, they are wrong, because Finn, Dalton and Micah are exactly why I agreed to help out. Those three boys are a handful, even when their parents aren't out of town."

Avalynne fell into step beside him, still skeptical, and laced her arm through his. "Cady's got a crush on you, you know. She's always had one."

Jeb wished that was the case. It would give him a boost in his pursuit of her. "Cady and I are friends," he said quietly, extricating his arm. *Although I wish it was more. I wish she would let me pursue her the way I want to, full out, with no holds barred....*

"Mmm-hmm." Avalynne waited on the porch while he locked the front door. When he turned back to her, she looked at him seriously and said, "Listen to me, Jeb. If Cady has what you've decided you want, don't ignore this chance. Give it—give her—the best you've got."

Jeb knew his former fiancée wanted him to find the kind of happiness she had apparently found for herself. "Thanks for the advice."

"You're welcome, pal." She touched his face, then stood on tiptoe and kissed the side of his jaw with the affection of an old friend.

Jeb waited while his ex drove away, then headed for his parents' ranch. As he expected, nothing was as simple as he would like it to be. But given the fact he had made the request, and his parents had agreed to assist, he was honor bound to help out. So, lamenting the time apart from Cady, he rolled up his sleeves and got to work.

To Jeb's surprise, Cady was waiting for him when he returned. She did not look happy. Tensing, he dropped his keys on the hall console. "What's the matter?"

She folded her arms in front of her. "We had a visitor while you were gone."

Jeb blinked. "This late?"

"*Mrs. Stone* felt it couldn't wait."

Avalynne's mother? Jeb felt a sinking sensation in his gut. He worked to keep from overreacting. "Was she looking for me?"

A muscle worked in Cady's jaw. "Actually, she knew where you were, since she had followed Avalynne from town to your place, and then waited while you two met up and slipped inside the Flying M ranch house."

Clearly, Cady imagined the worst.

Jeb lifted a staying hand. "I can explain." Part of it, anyway.

Cady glared at him. "Then perhaps you should do so to Mrs. Stone, because she thinks you are still leading her daughter on. And worse, keeping Avalynne from getting involved with anyone else."

Stiffening with resentment, Jeb met Cady's level glance. "That's not true."

She stepped closer, arms still clamped beneath her breasts. "But you were with Avalynne tonight," she ascertained, an accusing edge in her low tone.

While the male in him relished Cady's jealousy—because it meant she cared more than she wanted to admit—the stand-up guy deplored the implication that he would hop from one woman's arms into another's.

He grimaced. "Yes. I was," he replied honestly.

Cady leaned toward him, the fragrance of her perfume teasing his senses. "You knew you were going to see her but said nothing to me?"

He averted his glance. "It was private."

"I'll bet," she sniffed, a riot of pretty color flooding her high, sculpted cheeks.

Jeb turned his attention back to her face. How had he gone from making hot, wild love to Cady this afternoon, to dwelling on his past with another woman tonight?

Yet he knew enough about Cady to realize that until she was satisfied she was the only woman he wanted, nothing more would be possible between them. Probably not even friendship...

"Avalynne and I..."

"I gather the two of you still have a thing?" Turning away, she tossed her hair haughtily. "It really doesn't matter."

Like hell it didn't. He caught her by the shoulders and spun her back, willing her to listen to him. "It does matter if you're upset."

Cady scowled. "Why should I be upset? Just because you went from my bed..." Her cheeks turned even pinker, as her eyes blazed. "Well, we weren't exactly in the bedroom this afternoon. *Were we?*"

Now she was going to blame him for the eroticism of their encounter? "Only because you didn't want to go there." In fact, if it had been up to him, if they hadn't had other obligations—like the kids—they would still be there, wrapped in one another's arms. And maybe then she wouldn't be doubting him this way.

She lifted a hand dismissively. "You're free to hook up with anyone you want."

"I'm not involved with Avalynne."

"Then why are you meeting her secretly at your ranch late at night? Apparently, not just this time, but every time she comes to town."

Jeb rubbed his hand across his jaw. "There's a reason

we meet up that way," he said finally. "And it has nothing to do with romance or sex or anything else remotely like that."

Cady wanted to believe him; he could see it in her eyes. "Then what's it about?"

"A promise I made to her, many years ago."

Cady stared at him. "Is this some sort of payback for you leaving her at the altar?"

"More like the reverse," Jeb said reluctantly, torn between his own sense of honor and his need to keep Cady in his life.

Anxiety clouded her eyes, and she raked her teeth across her lip. "I don't understand."

Suddenly, the burden he had carried for years was unbearable. Jeb had to confide in someone. He wanted that person to be Cady. "I didn't leave Avalynne at the altar, Cady. She left me."

IT TOOK A FEW MOMENTS for the information to process. Cady stared at Jeb. "What are you talking about?"

Looking as if he wished the conversation had never started, he said, "Avalynne's the one who decided she didn't want to get married that day."

Cady made no effort to conceal her shock. "Why?" How was that even possible?

Jeb stepped closer, exuding heat and strength. "She found the whole idea of making a lifelong commitment suffocating." His handsome features tautening, he kept his eyes locked with Cody's. "She wanted to forget about the life we had planned here in Laramie and see the world...to use those experiences to inspire her creativity as an artist."

Which it had, Cady thought. Avalynne's paintings had sold worldwide.

"And she wanted you to run away with her," Cady guessed.

"No, she wanted to go off on her own," Jeb corrected with a disgruntled frown. "The two of us had been together since high school. Avalynne felt being with me that way had robbed her of the chance to truly experience life."

His expression was shuttered, but Cady could imagine how much that must have hurt, at the time. "That was really brutal."

He winced. "But honest."

Cady studied the suppressed emotion in his eyes. She stepped closer, her footsteps echoing on the marble floor of the foyer. "Were you having doubts, too?"

Jeb walked into the living room and sat down on the sofa. "I knew something was wrong. I chalked it up to prewedding jitters, and the pressure her parents—particularly her mother—was putting on her to have the perfect wedding and an even more perfect marriage."

Cady perched on the coffee table directly in front of him. "So you still wanted to get married." Unlike what everyone had always thought.

Jeb nodded, lowering his guard even more. He leaned forward, his hands clasped between his spread knees. "Until I found out Avalynne couldn't make that kind of commitment to me. Then, of course, I realized we couldn't go through with it. The ceremony would have been a lie."

Cady recalled the shock that had rippled through the chapel when Jeb had come out alone to address the guests that day. He had been so grim and ill at ease.

Now she knew why. None of this had been his doing. Had it been up to him, he'd be happily married now, with kids.

Her heart went out to him.

Idly, she fingered the stack of magazines next to her. "So why didn't you and Avalynne come out and tell everyone that you had jointly decided not to marry? It's not like that's never happened before. A lot of couples who decide not to tie the knot simply apologize to their guests, promise to return the gifts, and go on to the reception, anyway. I mean—" she lifted her hands, palms up, "—why let a party that's already been set up and paid for go to waste?"

A sensual light gleamed in Jeb's eyes. His lips curved ruefully. "You're right." He regarded her pragmatically. "That would have been my choice. To make the best of a bad situation, show everyone that even though Avalynne and I weren't getting married that day, we had decided we could still be friends."

"But you didn't do that," Cady recalled.

He sighed and sat back against the cushions. "Avalynne knew her parents would never forgive her if she told them she'd had any part in backing out of a settled, respectable life as a married woman in Laramie, Texas. And she wanted a reasonable excuse to leave immediately and jump on a plane to Europe. So," Jeb recounted with a mixture of acceptance and regret, "she asked me if I would cover for her and take the blame."

Oh, no, Cady thought.

He compressed his lips, admitting, "At the time, I figured it was not that big a deal. That people would be upset with me, for a time. And then it would all blow over."

Except it hadn't.

"So I promised her I would keep the truth about what happened a secret," Jeb continued.

Which wasn't a surprise, Cady knew, since—like all the McCabe men—Jeb was honorable to the core.

"And maybe all the talk would have died down," she mused aloud, "had Avalynne's parents not sued you for the cost of the wedding."

Jeb let his head fall back against the cushions and ran his hands through his hair. "Yeah. That was a real mess." He flexed the taut muscles in his broad shoulders and clasped his entwined hands behind his neck. "I had to take out a loan to pay them back."

Cady moved over onto the sofa to sit facing him. She touched his biceps empathetically. "I can't believe Avalynne let you take the fall for that."

The distant look was back in Jeb's eyes. "She didn't know about it. She was backpacking through Europe by then."

It upset Cady to see him letting Avalynne off the hook, even now. "You could have told everyone the truth then," she pointed out.

Jeb stood and began to pace. "I had no interest in that kind of confrontation, with or without Avalynne present," he said in a low, brooding tone. He stopped next to the marble fireplace, examining the photos Suki had lined up on the mantel. "It would have been a lot uglier than what happened at the church, and that was bad enough. Besides—" he turned back to Cady and exhaled deeply "—I knew Avalynne would settle up with me, when she found out what her parents had done." He came toward Cady once again, his expression as forthright as ever. "And she did. She insisted she foot the bill for the entire botched wedding. And she's been quietly paying me back ever since, a few thousand dollars at a time."

Cady conceded that was the decent thing for his ex to do. As for the rest...

She stood, facing off with him once again. "Is that why you've been meeting secretly with her every time she comes to town?"

Jeb nodded. "It'd be a lot easier if she could just pay it all off in one lump sum. But her dad's CPA firm does her taxes and there's no way Avalynne could explain an exorbitant amount like that." He added stoically, "So she has no choice but to keep withdrawing the money from her bank account a little at a time, and then stores the cash in a safety deposit box."

Aware that the fragrance of his soap and skin were engendering fantasies of what it would be like to be in his arms again, Cady stepped back and sighed. "Sounds like Avalynne is still very much under her parents' thumb."

Jeb scrubbed a hand across his jaw. "That's just the way it is when she's in Texas, which may be why she is always traveling and working overseas. So she won't have to deal with their interference."

Cady studied the complex mix of emotions in Jeb's eyes. Glad he was letting her be there for him, the way he had been there for her the last few days, she regarded him soberly. "And you've never told anyone this, not even your parents?"

"I've been tempted, but..." He paused, the brooding look back on his handsome face. "I know they would be disappointed to find out I ever lied about what went down that day in the first place. They would have wanted me to tell the truth and take my lumps, not have this continuing stain on my reputation."

Cady edged nearer. "They'd be right."

Jeb shrugged and looked down at her. "I know what we bet—that if I made it the whole two weeks you'd have to use your powers as a marketing rep to make this whole thing go away—but the truth is, aside from the occasional irritation, it hasn't really hurt me."

"Sure about that?" Cady responded swiftly, feeling just as protective toward Jeb as he did toward her. "It's the fact that you supposedly left Avalynne at the altar—and hence, humiliated her in front of the entire community—that has you on the 'Men to Avoid Getting Romantically Entangled with' list. It's one of the primary things that's keeping you from attracting all the truly marriageable women in Laramie County."

Decade-long resignation warred with irritation on his face. "And you're worried about that?"

Maybe, Cady thought.

Sensing he needed comforting, as any friend would in this situation, she reached over and took his hand. The warmth of their entwined fingers spread up her arm as she gazed into his eyes. "Shouldn't *you* be?" she murmured.

Jeb tightened his hand on hers, and let his smoldering gaze rove over her upswept hair and her face before returning, ever so slowly and deliberately, to her eyes.

"If that misconception is what is keeping you and me apart, then you're right," he finished huskily. "I damn well should be."

Chapter Nine

Was Jeb right? Was this misconception what was keeping them apart? Cady wondered. Or was it more?

"First and foremost, you and I are friends, Jeb." And she had promised herself she would never allow herself to become romantically entangled with any man who put her in the "just friends" category. Whether at the beginning of their relationship or the end, it didn't matter—either way spelled doom.

Incredulity mixed with concern on Jeb's face. "And friends can't commit to anything beyond friendship, is that what you're saying?" he countered, frustration curling his lips.

Of course they could, but... Still standing directly in front of him, Cady braced herself in challenge. "The only relationships I've seen last are ones that have a foundation of passionate, abiding love. That's what my sister has with her husband. It's what I want for myself," Cady continued, determined to be honest and let him know where they stood. "I'm not going to settle, and you shouldn't, either." She waved a reproving finger. "Particularly since you'd be married now if Avalynne hadn't walked out on you."

Jeb lounged against the foyer wall. In deference to

the boys sleeping just upstairs, he kept his voice low, yet there was nothing amenable about his gaze. "Married and divorced, most likely." In his view, what might or might not have happened ten years ago changed nothing now.

Cady drew a deep breath and headed for the kitchen. "The point is," she murmured, "you wanted marriage and family before you had your heart tromped on." He caught up with her as she passed the first floor powder room. Aware of his closeness, she tipped her gaze up to his. "You could want it all again."

He tilted his head to study her, looking more determined than ever to make her his—at least once more—before this joint babysitting gig ended.

Ignoring the reckless warmth spiraling through her, Cady pushed aside the desire and held her ground. "All it's going to take is you meeting the right woman, the one who'll make you feel that anything and everything is possible again."

Jeb shrugged, then leaned closer once again, bringing with him the tantalizing fragrance of his cologne. "Maybe I already have."

Cady lifted a brow, waited. Suddenly, she was having trouble getting her breath.

"Being around you and the boys the last few days has caused me to do a lot of thinking." His voice dropped a seductive notch. "It's made me realize I do want a wife and kids." He paused and looked deep into her eyes, adding even more softly, "Maybe more than I ever knew."

Wanting family was different than wanting her, specifically, as his bride and the mother of his children. Regardless, Cady felt a thrill go through her. Along with the wish that somehow, some way, she would find herself in the running as the woman who would one day steal Jeb's heart.

"Well, see, then you're there," she said lightly, returning to the safety of her laptop computer and the distraction it always offered. What seemed so perfect to the two of them now might not seem so ideal once they were relieved of the challenging responsibility of the three boys, and were no longer living beneath the same roof. And Cady was too smart and cautious to let either of them get swept up in false intimacy.

She glimpsed the flashing icon, sat down, and opened up her mailbox. There was a message with an attachment from TinaMatthews @ TheStorkAgency.com.

Eagerly, Cady began to read.

Hey, Cady,
The doc took this photo of Zoe today, and I figured you'd like to see it. Isn't she AWESOME? I'm probably going to deliver in the next ten to fourteen days. I hope you're still planning to come to the hospital and be there for the BIG MOMENT.
Luv ya,
Tina Matthews

Cady's hands trembled as she clicked on the attachment.

Inside was a color photo of Zoe floating in a halo of light, arms folded in front of her, legs curled up against her body. She had her eyes closed tight, a slightly annoyed expression on her face, and she was the most beautiful baby Cady had ever seen.

Cady stared at the photo a second longer, then began to type a response.

Tina,
You're right—Zoe is awesome! And yes, I am planning to be there for the birth. I wouldn't miss it for the world. In the meantime, take care, and let me know if there is anything I can do for you. I'll be thinking of you.
Fondly,
Cady

JEB HAD NEVER SEEN so many expressions cross Cady's face in one minute. Caution. Wariness. Joy. And now happiness mixed with relief.

"Everything okay?"

Nodding, she leaped from her chair and bounded toward the front of the house. "Come with me." She raced down the hall and led the way to Hermann's study. The printer was humming, a page already spitting out. Cady picked it up, smiling again, and handed it over. "Look what Zoe just sent me!"

Jeb surveyed the color photo of a baby in utero.

"It's Zoe, Jeb. Isn't she amazing?"

She was. So much so, in fact, that Jeb couldn't take his eyes off the baby, who was so far along in her development she looked ready to be born right now. He found himself smiling affectionately, too, at the scowling cherub. "She looks ticked off."

"That's what I thought." Cady beamed, the reality of the photo bringing an even more blissful tenor to the moment. She leaned in close to continue to study the picture, her head resting against Jeb's shoulder. "She probably doesn't like having her picture taken."

He wrapped an arm around Cady's waist and drew her closer yet. "Apparently not."

Tears suddenly shimmered in Cady's eyes. "I can't believe it, Jeb," she whispered emotionally, her slender body trembling in excitement. "I'm *finally* going to be able to adopt a baby. It's really going to happen! This picture proves it!"

Did it? Jeb pushed his unease away.

"She asked me to come to the hospital and be there for the birth, too."

Jeb watched Cady go back to the printer for a second page. "When is Tina due?"

"In ten to fourteen days."

"In other words, right after Suki and Hermann get back," he stated.

Cady rushed back to his side. "Pretty much." She handed over the second page. "She sent me this message, too." She pointed where she wanted him to read. "There's my reply."

Jeb scanned both emails, the niggling uncertainty deep inside him increasing. Aware Cady wanted him to say something, he tried to be as circumspect as possible. "She seems very excited."

"Most new moms are. But not..." Cady frowned as her next thought hit "...ones who are about to give up their baby." Abruptly, she sat down on the edge of Hermann's heavy mahogany desk.

Jeb put the photo and correspondence aside. He rested a comforting hand on Cady's slender shoulder and forced himself to look at the situation in another way. "It could be all bravura. Tina Matthews is a teenager. And teens like to act as if they have it all together, even when they don't. Or maybe," he added with a crooked smile, "*especially* when they don't."

Cady sagged in relief. She gazed up at him, comforted by the thought. "You're right," she replied sagely, getting up off the desk once again. She picked up the pages and brushed by him. "Tina's had months to speak to the counselors and think about what she's doing. No doubt this email she sent me is just another way of coping, of telling herself what she is doing is all for the best."

CADY FELL ASLEEP with Zoe's ultrasound photo in her hands, and awakened with a toddler curled up beside her. Micah had climbed in bed with her during the night. Knowing how much he missed his mom, she'd let him stay.

Contentment flowed through her as Micah snuggled even closer. Cady wondered if this was how it would be when she adopted Zoe. If the little girl would seek her out in the middle of the night, too.

"Here he is!" Dalton shouted in glee.

"Our Friend Jeb! We found our baby brother!" Finn added. He barreled in next, and together, the two boys zipped across the room and hopped onto the foot of Cady's bed.

Jeb appeared in the doorway, looking as if he'd just awakened. "Sorry," he said. "The boys told me Micah wasn't in his bed. They were a little panicked."

Cady tore her eyes from his low slung pajama pants and bare chest. Damn, but he was attractive. "That's perfectly understandable." The sight of his sculpted pecs and the mat of sexy golden hair arrowing past his navel made her pulse pound and her throat go dry.

"How come he gets to sleep in here?" Dalton pouted.

"Yeah, I want to sleep in here," Finn declared as he snuggled up to Cady, too.

She thanked heaven for little chaperones who would keep her on track. Watching over them, Jeb smiled fondly.

"What about you, Jeb?" Dalton piped up, joining the group cuddle session with Cady.

Mischief glimmered in Jeb's eyes. "I wouldn't mind."

Cady imagined he wouldn't....

Oblivious to the sudden, sexy detour of the adults' thoughts, the two older boys bounced on the bed. "Hey, wake up, Micah!" they shouted with typical exuberance.

The toddler slowly and reluctantly opened his eyes, then scrambled upright as if he had never been asleep. "Hungry," he said.

"We're hungry, too," his brothers complained in unison.

Once again, Jeb swooped in to the rescue. "How about I change Micah's diaper and get all three of them breakfast?"

Was he doing this because he was kind, or because it was her birthday? Cady couldn't tell. The only thing she knew for sure was that no one had mentioned it was her big day. Thus far, anyway.

She was being silly to feel even the slightest bit disappointed, she thought minutes later, as she stood in the shower, letting the warm water sluice over her.

She had asked everyone—including her friends

back in Houston—to let her birthday go unnoticed this year.

No parties. No gifts, either—although Suki and Hermann had already ignored that entreaty with the package they'd had delivered the other day.

And no mention of it until she had adopted her baby and was ready to celebrate turning thirty-four.

She'd gotten exactly what she had told Jeb that she wanted, Cady realized, as she turned off the water and wrapped herself in a luxurious bath towel.

So why was she suddenly depressed?

UNFORTUNATELY, her day went from bad to worse. No sooner had Cady walked into the kitchen to join the guys for breakfast than her cell phone went off. One glance at the in-box showed half a dozen text messages, another dozen missed calls.

The VPs at Hanover Horseshoes had moved up the delivery date on the marketing plan. The spokesmodel everyone had agreed was perfect for the gig had just landed a part in a movie filming in Mexico, and was no longer available. A conference call was scheduled for nine-thirty, and Cady was expected to be on it, vacation or no vacation.

"It's not a problem," Jeb said. "I'll take the boys for the day and we'll meet up at my place for dinner, say around five o'clock?"

Cady looked at all she had to do and groaned in abject misery. "Better make that six…."

He wrapped an arm around her shoulders and squeezed with the affection of an old friend, instead of a boyfriend-to-be. "See you then…."

Trying not to think about how easily Jeb was able to

let go of their lovemaking, and how much she wished it could happen again, Cady settled down to work. By the time she finished, it was nearly five-thirty.

She went upstairs to freshen up, then called Jeb to let him know she was on her way. She could hear the boys in the background. "Tell Aunt Cady to hurry up!" Dalton yelled.

"Yeah," Finn agreed loudly, "we can't wait for her to—"

The sound cut off abruptly, as Jeb apparently covered the phone. When he came back on, there was dead silence—except for some telltale giggles—in the background.

Wondering what was going on, Cady asked, "Everything okay?"

"They're just excited to see you," Jeb said matter-of-factly.

Cady had missed them, too.

Although it sounded as if they had had a very good time without her.

She grabbed her purse and keys. "I'll be there in five."

Minutes later, when she pulled up in front of Jeb's ranch house, all three boys were seated on the front steps. Jeb was standing next to them.

"You're not going to believe what's behind the house!" Dalton leaped up to greet her.

"Aunt Cady! In there!" Micah pointed to the front door.

Finn rushed to take her hand. "You're going to love it, Aunt Cady."

"But first," five-year-old Dalton instructed, more seriously than ever, "you have to close your eyes."

Cady glanced at Jeb. He looked pretty proud of himself, she noted.

"Better do as they say," he told her solemnly as he grasped Cady's other arm.

She closed her eyes and let them steer her toward the front door, while the other boys raced on ahead.

"Keep your eyes closed, Aunt Cady!" Finn told her.

"Yeah, we'll tell you when you can open them!" Dalton cried.

Cady obeyed as she was led blindly through the hall, into the kitchen and out onto the screened in back porch.

"Okay, you can open your eyes now!" The boys' excited voices tumbled over each other.

She did. And could barely believe what she saw.

"It's a princess birthday party!" Finn told her. Complete with birthday presents, cake and a huge bouncy-house castle in the backyard.

Beaming, her nephews handed her a glittery gold tiara and a pink-and-white, faux-fur trimmed cape. "Do you like it?"

A lump rising in her throat, Cady settled the "robe" around her shoulders and sat down in shock. "I love it."

The boys clapped their hands. "Well, then, you're really going to *love* the presents we got you, too. Get it?" Finn handed her a gift.

Jeb chuckled. "Better open it," he advised Cady drily. "Before they expire with excitement."

Cady worked off the paper. Inside was a white wooden sculpture of the word *Love*.

"See?" Finn said. "Don't you love it?"

"I do."

"Open mine," Dalton insisted.

Inside was a necklace of pink plastic beads. "It's pink. So it's a girl color," he explained happily.

Cady slipped it around her neck. "It is. And I love it, too."

Micah held out his gift. Cady opened it and found a soft pink-and-white chiffon scarf. She smiled and took the two-year-old into her arms for a hug. "I love this, too," she told the beaming child.

"We've got more!" The boys raced off, returning with three small framed canvases. "This is you and us, Aunt Cady," Dalton explained, showing her his stick figures.

"This is you and Our Friend Jeb." Finn handed her his drawing.

Micah gave her his. "Flowers," he said shyly.

"They are all wonderful." Cady was deeply touched. "I'm going to take them home and hang them in my loft."

The boys grinned wider, then turned to Jeb. "Aren't you going to give her your present?"

He smiled and reached for a small box in the center of the table. "The boys helped me pick this out, too," he said.

Cady opened it.

Inside was a bottle of Pretty Princess bubble bath. She wasn't sure whether to be amused or hurt. But she wasn't going to disappoint the boys after all their hard work.

"Got to love it," she said of the bubble bath, telling herself such a gift from Jeb was for the best. "In fact—" she smiled and held her arms out to embrace all three of her nephews and Jeb in a heartfelt group hug "—I love it all."

If she wanted more from her relationship with Jeb... that was a matter for another time.

"BELIEVE IT OR NOT, they're all asleep," Jeb reported several hours later. In a knit shirt and jeans, his sandy-brown hair rumpled and the hint of five o'clock shadow on his face, he looked sexy and at home.

And all Cady could think about was what it would be like if she and Jeb lived together like this all the time.

Certainly, he made everything fun and exciting. Not just for the boys, but for her, too.

She pulled a load of towels from the dryer, carried them into the family room and upended the basket on the sofa. "You were up there only five minutes."

He sauntered over to help her fold. "That bouncy house really wore them out."

The easy camaraderie, plus his willingness to help, warmed her even more. She slanted him an appreciative glance. "Thanks for the party."

A deadpan grin creased his face. "I know you didn't want one. I tried explaining that to the boys, but the idea of your birthday going by without a celebration was not something they could sanction."

Cady could only imagine the howls of protest that would have engendered.

"So..." Jeb shrugged his broad shoulders amiably. "We went with it and gave you the best princess birthday party we could dream up."

Chuckling, Cady folded the last towel and placed the stack into the basket. Setting it aside, she propped her hands on her hips and gushed, "I have to say, it was fantastic."

Jeb sauntered closer and gazed at her as if she were the sexiest, most desirable woman on earth. "And now," he said softly, pausing to look deep into her eyes, "for the real birthday present from me."

Cady's heart accelerated to a thunderous beat.

He pulled a small, square jewelry box out of his pants pocket.

"You didn't have to do this," she whispered, enthralled.

His eyes gleamed with undisguised affection. "I wanted to."

She had only to look at him to see that was true.

Gulping, she opened the velvet box.

Inside, nestled in a bed of satin, was a gold, heart-shaped locket.

Jeb leaned closer. "You can put your baby's photo in there."

Actually, she could fit two photos inside. Unbidden, the images of the baby and Jeb appeared simultaneously. Cady drew a breath and shut her eyes. She really was getting ridiculously sentimental. Maybe because when she was with Jeb like this, she felt as if all her dreams were about to come true.

Looking just as content, he took the necklace and stepped behind her, leaning down to murmur in her ear. "I'll help you try it on."

Trembling all over, she lifted her hair off the nape of her neck, to assist him. His hands brushed her skin as he fastened the clasp and settled the locket at her throat. She released her hair as he came back around to view his handiwork. "Well, what do you know—" pleasure lifted the corners of his lips "—it matches your tiara."

Cady reached for it. She had forgotten that was still on her head. "Whoops…"

He stopped her with his hand over hers. "Leave it on," he ordered huskily, his gaze drifting over her ardently before returning with slow deliberation to her face. "I like the way you look…."

Suddenly, she wasn't the only one with illicit longings. The need to be touched, held, loved. "Jeb…"

He cupped her face and tilted her lips to his. A wealth of feeling was in his eyes. "Let me kiss you, Cady," he implored. "Just one kiss."

Cady should have said no. Would have said no. But it was her birthday after all…and his will was fiercer than hers. "Okay," she conceded, closing her eyes. "But just one…"

The only problem was, there was no stopping with one. For either of them. The moment his lips captured hers, the last of her resistance melted, then faded entirely. A volcano of desire erupted inside her. The next thing she knew, he was sweeping her up into his arms and carrying her toward the stairs.

He stopped to kiss her again, on the landing. And again when they reached the upstairs hall. And then there was no more delaying as he strode toward the guest room where he was residing.

He set her down near the bed, then walked over to shut and lock the door. As he came back to her, Cady's heart took on an even more erratic beat.

"Happy birthday," Jeb whispered, taking her in his arms once again.

Standing there in the splash of moonlight with

him, it felt like the best ever. Cady couldn't help but chuckle. "You're certainly making it a day to remember, cowboy."

He favored her with a lopsided grin, then kissed her leisurely. Determined to savor every instant of their coming together, she kissed him back. He unbuttoned her blouse, let it fall to the floor. She slid his knit shirt over his head and drew it off.

Her breasts tautened as her bra went the way of her shirt. "You are so beautiful," he murmured, his fingertips brushing the sides of her bare breasts.

She felt beautiful when he looked at her that way, all hot and bothered. Never wanting their lovemaking to stop, she took his wrists and guided his hands to cup her breasts. His callused palms were warm against her skin. A shiver went through her and she caught her breath as another wave of yearning swept through her. There was no hiding how much he wanted her, no denying his need as he flicked his thumbs over the very tips of her nipples.

Something was happening here, something that could potentially change both their lives.

Her back arched, her hips pressing against the hardness of his. He anchored her upright, with an arm about her waist. Still cupping her breast, he slowly kissed his way down her throat to her collarbone, then lower still. The rough, wild rasp of his tongue, combined with the gentle suckling, caused her knees to buckle.

He chuckled in satisfaction and, still holding her, lowered her to the bed. Her shorts and his jeans were in the way. With mounting impatience, they got rid of them. Undergarments followed. He slid between her thighs, the rhythmic pressure of his hands and his mouth taking her to new heights, making her burn inside.

And he burned for her, too. Cady made sure of it as she wriggled out from beneath him. Daring more than she ever had, she took the lead. Touching, stroking, taking him all for her own.

As he slid inside her and they finally came together, she regretted all the times she had cut off her feelings. All the times she had chosen the mask of friendship over the risk of love. Jeb wasn't in love with her, even though she might be very close to falling in love with him. But right now it didn't matter. They were together, as one.

She was taking him into her very depths and he was transporting her to a place unlike anywhere she had ever been. To a place that was soft and warm and sexy. A place that made her feel so very wanted, and so very much alive. And for tonight, she thought tenderly, as they both plummeted over the edge, it was more than enough.

Chapter Ten

The first time Jeb and Cady made love had been an amazing surprise. A way to distract themselves from the chaos of caring for the kids, satisfy their growing curiosity about one another and find comfort in each other's arms. The second time was like coming home. And as Cady cuddled against him, Jeb sensed she was just as content.

He kissed her shoulder, loving the way she felt against him, so soft and naked and warm. And then he felt her tense.

Cady lifted her head. Confusion warred with the quiet deliberation on her face. "I promised myself I wouldn't let this happen again."

He touched a hand to her hair, burying his fingers in the silky softness. He knew what she presumed, as she struggled to keep this on a strictly practical level. That it was just about sex. But it wasn't, he thought, as he rolled to his side and shifted her to lie facing him. Their hearts and minds and souls had been engaged from the very first. They just hadn't allowed themselves to act on any of their feelings, for fear it would ruin what had been a damn fine friendship.

He trailed a palm over the indentation of her waist,

the curve of her hip. "But we did." He watched her lips part softly in response. "Maybe there's a reason for that," he continued, kissing her temple tenderly.

Cady closed her eyes briefly and hitched in a breath. "Like what?" she whispered.

He stroked the satiny skin of her breasts, letting her know he was still as wild for her as she was for him. Bent to kiss the tempting roundness, then the tip.

Deliberately avoiding the part of her he most wanted to touch, he moved upward and captured her lips once more. He kissed her until she moaned, a little helpless sound that sent his senses swimming, and then opened her lips even more.

And yet when the kiss ended, some resistance remained, along with the partially in place barbed wire around her heart. So he cupped her chin in his hand. "It's like we're meant to be more than just friends…"

"Friends with benefits?" Skepticism laced her low tone. She started to leave the bed.

Okay, maybe not that. Cursing himself for not having realized it was the wrong thing to say, he caught her wrist and drew her back.

The truth was, the passion they felt for each other aside, he was just as confused as she was.

After his botched engagement, he hadn't planned ever to allow himself to be truly vulnerable or get emotionally involved with a woman again. Friends were in the equation. So were fun and sex.

But the categories were separate. The boundaries clear-cut. So clear-cut he had earned a well-deserved reputation as bad marriage material.

Although he still had no interest in marriage per se, he did have a desire to be with Cady. To turn his long-held fantasies about her into everyday reality. Not just the occasional "sexy mistake."

He studied the resistant posture of her slender frame. Maybe she just needed him to slow things down, take it a little easier. "Hey." He caught her hand, and held it over his heart. "We don't have to figure out everything tonight."

Cady turned wary eyes to him and drew a quavering breath. Her pulse was pounding as rapidly as his. "Then when? I'm only going to be in Laramie another week." She shook her head, rushing on in a troubled tone. "After that, I'm back in Houston. I'm adopting a baby. I'll be juggling motherhood and work—"

He pressed a silencing finger against her lips. "We can make time to be together if that's what we both want. I'll even do all the traveling." It would be a privilege to do so, if it meant he'd be with her, instead of just thinking about it.

She let out a shuddering sigh. "You say that now."

He wrapped his arms around her and brought her against him. "I mean it now." He searched her face, letting her know with a long look that he would give her the space she apparently needed. "We don't have to do the usual thing...don't have to be married...to be happy together." He did his best to put a practical spin on the situation, one that Cady could accept. "All we have to do to make this work is enjoy being together when we have the chance."

Determined to show her just how important she had become to him, how resolved he was to find a way to give her everything she needed and wanted in a relationship, Jeb positioned her on her back once again. He slipped between her thighs, prepared to be relentless in his pursuit of her.

Still holding her gently, he ran his tongue along the seam of her lips, until they parted in surrender and she curled against him, wanting more.

"We can set our own parameters and make our own rules. Just the way you're doing in adopting a baby on your own." He delivered sweet, seductive kisses that had both their bodies heating. "We can find our own happiness, Cady. And we can do it together...."

Her breasts pearled against his chest. She rubbed her body against his, all soft feminine pliability and need. Jeb moaned deep and low in his throat as she kissed him back.

"You're right," she murmured, "I am overthinking this. And I do—" her amber eyes lit up wickedly "—want to make love with you again."

Palm to his chest, she pushed him onto his back and climbed astride him. She clasped his shoulders and kissed her way down his chest.

"My turn to take charge," she whispered playfully.

Luxuriating in the hot, sexy feel of her, he ran his hands over her silky skin, then captured her breasts with his hands. "For a while," he agreed with an unrepentant smile.

Laughing smoothly, she moved lower still, her hair brushing his abdomen and thighs.

Basking in the sweet smell of her body, and the lingering fragrance of her perfume, he knew she was everything he had ever needed. She'd brought him deftly out of the disappointment of the past, and into the here and now, to a place where enduring happiness not only seemed possible, but probable....

The gentle eroticism of her lovemaking flowed through him, fulfilling every fantasy he'd ever had. The need to possess her built to a fierce, unquenchable ache. Determined to make this as good for her as it was for him, he swiftly traded places with her, kissing and loving every feminine inch of her, not stopping until she was calling his name, coming apart in his hands.

With satisfaction roaring through him as strongly as his need, Jeb moved upward once again. He kissed her fully, deeply, until their bodies took up a primitive rhythm all on their own and there was no doubting how much they wanted to mesh. Stretching over her, he slid his palms beneath her and lifted her in his hands. With a wild cry, she arched against him, opened herself up to him. His heart pounding, his spirits soaring, he dived into slick, hot velvet, to the welcoming warmth inside, knowing she was everything he had ever wanted in a woman and more. And then he was pressing into her as deeply as he could go, discovering their pleasure, taking her to incredible heights with him, again and again. After the last shuddering spasm finally passed, they clung to each other in sheer contentment and lay cocooned in one another's arms.

THE LAST THING Cady wanted after making love with Jeb the second time was to leave his bed. But she knew, for all their sakes, she had to go.

With a sigh, she disentangled herself from the warm seduction of his arms and sat up.

"The boys can't find us together like this," she told him reluctantly. "I have to go back to my own room."

Jeb squeezed her hand. "You're right," he agreed, with a sigh of regret and another brief, tender kiss. "It would be too confusing for them. But as soon as this babysitting gig is over—" he winked, reluctantly letting her go "—you owe me a full night in my arms."

The image he conjured up brought forth another wave of desire.

Aware she was getting in too deep, too fast, she chose to misunderstand the reason behind the offer by teasing. "That wasn't the payoff for our bet." Cady rose and slipped on her undies. "Which, I'm pained to admit, given the staying power you have exhibited in the substitute-daddy department, you are likely to win."

Jeb got up and assisted with the clasp of her bra. "Forget the payoff, Cady." He shifted her hair and bent to kiss her nape. Hands on her shoulders, he turned her to face him. "And forget the bet." He cupped her face and regarded her tenderly. "And just think about us. The way we are right now. I can't get enough of you, Cady." He kissed her again. "And the way things are going, I don't think I ever will."

His words stayed with her as she fell asleep. They were still with her as she awakened six hours later, when Micah toddled sleepily into her room and crawled in bed with her. Two minutes later, a rambunctious Finn and Dalton followed, with a sluggish, sexy-looking Jeb on their heels.

Cady sat up, aware that beneath her cotton pj's, she felt very well loved. Emotionally, well, she felt adored. She sat up against the headboard and held out her arms for the usual exuberant hugs. "Good morning, guys!"

"Mornin', Aunt Cady!" Micah commandeered Cady's lap, while Finn and Dalton snuggled at her sides. Jeb grinned at the cozy scene and sat on the end of the bed, looking every bit as content as Cady felt.

"So what's on the schedule for today?" he asked with a grin.

Thanks to the time given her the day before, Cady was all caught up on her work. She doubted the same could be said of Jeb. "I know you must have a lot to do at your ranch. Why don't you go ahead and see to that? I'll watch the boys today. We'll meet up later, when you're done."

"That would be great." He stood and surveyed the bed like a king looking over his kingdom. "How about dinner at my place again tonight?"

The boys cheered. "Will the bouncy castle still be there?" Finn demanded.

Jeb nodded. "The crew won't be back to get it until tomorrow."

"So we can play on it again?"

He nodded. "For one more day."

"Hurrah…!"

Because he had so much to do, Jeb dressed, said goodbye to everyone and took off.

Cady fixed the boys breakfast and then settled them in the family room, in front of their favorite video. She figured they wouldn't get into trouble in the ten minutes it would take her to shower and dress. And happily, when she had finished, they were just as she had left them, immersed in the TV.

Cady took the opportunity to check her email.

For once, things at work seemed okay.

A new spokesmodel had been found and put under contract. Cady's proposed marketing plan had been approved by her bosses and the Hanover Horseshoes VPs.

It was the email from Tina she found puzzling—and to be honest, a little unnerving.

Cady studied the pregnant teen's request a little while longer before she replied, wondering what Jeb would make of it....

"YOU'RE A HARD MAN to track down."

Jeb turned at the sound of his father's voice. Shane McCabe was standing at the pasture gate.

"Hey, Dad." He finished pounding in the loose fence post, then picked up his toolbox and walked to the next one. "What brings you here?"

"A couple of things." Shane fell into step beside him. "First, I wanted to see if you had decided whether to purchase a bull or go the IVF route to expand your breeding operation."

Jeb imagined his dad had lots of opinions on that, but this was something he wanted to decide himself. "I haven't had time to think about it yet."

Disapproval shone on Shane's face, as if he felt Jeb was letting his work slide.

"Second, Avalynne Stone's mother came to see your mom and me."

Jeb scowled. "Let me guess—she told you something illicit is going on between Avalynne and me."

Shane's eyebrows rose. "Is it?"

Jeb straightened the fence post, and gave it a hard whack. "What do you think?"

His dad stepped back. "That's not an answer."

Jeb glared at him. "I shouldn't have to answer that."

Shane folded his arms. "Need I remind you that you hurt Avalynne and her family enough, years ago, when you called off the wedding?"

Jeb resumed pounding, then moved to check out the

next post. It seemed sturdy enough, but he gave it a couple hard whacks anyway, driving it farther into the ground. "I have no intention of hurting her again."

"Mrs. Stone is convinced otherwise. Particularly since you're now involved with Cady Keilor, too."

Jeb tensed. He wiped the sweat dripping down his brow with the sleeve of his shirt. "Where did you hear that?"

Shane tipped up the brim of his hat. "Everyone in town is talking about the fact you've been sleeping over with Cady and her nephews."

So what? "I'm helping out," Jeb stated calmly.

"And trying to win a bet and God knows what else."

Jeb had done nothing to warrant being treated like a randy teenager. He swaggered on to the next post. "If this is leading up to a sex talk, I think we had that years ago."

His dad followed. "Do we need to have it again now?"

Aware he was about to lose his temper, Jeb tightened his grip on his toolbox and headed back to the barn. "You know I don't discuss my private affairs. Period."

"And normally," Shane agreed, keeping pace, "I would not ask you to, but these are both local women with continuing ties to the community. Avalynne doesn't live in Texas anymore, but Cady does, and she especially stands to be hurt if…"

"If what, Dad?" Jeb asked, knowing the actions of his family were fodder for gossip statewide. They stalked into the shadowy barn and back to the tool and tack room. "If she hooks up with one of the legendary Texas McCabes and it doesn't work out, then people will blame me and think less of me than they already do?" He took off his gloves and went over to wash his hands in the sink.

"If you lead Cady Keilor to think whatever this is could turn into something else, and then bail on her, the way you have every other woman in your life," Shane corrected, shadowing him every step of the way, "then yes, Cady stands to be hurt."

Jeb grabbed a paper towel. "Wow, Dad. You don't pull any punches, do you?"

"Your mother and I have made no secret of the fact that we think it's past time you stop sowing your wild oats and settle down. Because let's face it, marrying— for life—is the only way you will ever repair your reputation."

His back to the door, Jeb faced his father skeptically. "And who am I supposed to do this with—Avalynne?"

"No. With Cady. It's clear she's in love with you. She would be the kind of loyal, steadfast and caring wife you need."

"Whoa," Jeb interrupted, resenting the presumption. "Who said anything about love?" Cady certainly hadn't! "Don't you think you're rushing things a bit?" Not to mention interfering! Although his dad was right about one thing, Jeb admitted reluctantly. Cady was a wonderful woman, and exactly what he wanted and needed in a lifelong partner....

"I know this." Shane's lips tightened in mounting disapproval. "If you don't honor Cady with the attention and commitment she deserves, you will lose her, the way you've lost every other good woman who has come your way. And that would be—"

Shane stopped speaking abruptly.

Jeb looked at the chagrined expression on his face, then turned in the direction of the older man's gaze.

And swore silently to himself. Of all the people to be standing within earshot!

A pink-cheeked Cady lifted an apologetic hand. "I'm sorry. I didn't mean to interrupt you. I just wanted to tell you that the boys and I are here a lot earlier than you probably expected."

Several hours, in fact, Jeb noted. Glad for the disruption, he asked, "Where are they?"

Cady flashed a smile that did not reach her pretty eyes. "In the bouncy castle. They've been begging me nonstop all morning, since they know it's only going to be here for one more day, so I thought I would let them enjoy it. But—" she raised her slender hand again, already backing off "—if this is a bad time, I can round them up and take them to the park instead."

"Actually, it's not—I was just leaving," Shane smiled back, tipping his hat in respect. "Nice to see you, Cady."

She flushed, and this time her smile did reach her eyes. "Nice to see you, Mr. McCabe," she said shyly.

Cady waited until Shane had left, then turned back to Jeb. "I am sorry for interrupting."

"How much did you overhear?"

"Enough to know that your parents think you need to settle down and get serious about a woman, pronto, as a way of repairing your reputation. They're worried about you breaking my heart or leading me on—"

"I'm not going to do that," Jeb interrupted.

"But, given a choice, they'd prefer to see you end up with me, or maybe someone like me, rather than

Avalynne," Cady continued quietly, her uncertainty apparent.

He stepped closer, so their bodies were only an inch apart, and regarded her for a long, thoughtful moment. "First of all, as you well know, I've already made my choice."

"Have you, now?"

"I have." He met her level, challenging look. "And I made it even before we made love. You're the woman I want, Cady. The only woman." Cupping her shoulders, he paused to let his words sink in. "And I hope I'm the only man for you, too."

Her eyes softened in sweet surrender. "We're talking…?"

Jeb's pulse pounded as he recalled the uninhibited way she had given herself to him. "Becoming exclusive. Up till now, I guess I took it for granted—"

"Yes." Cady cut in with a grin before he even had a chance to finish the question.

He wrapped his arms around her, brought her close and kissed her tenderly, aware he was one step closer to having everything he wanted in his grasp. "I'm glad you agree."

Cady sighed contentedly. "Me, too." She splayed her hands across his chest, holding him at bay, the uncertainty back in her pretty amber eyes. "But there's another reason I came over so early, Jeb." She paused and bit her lip. "I have yet another favor to ask you. Tina emailed me a little while ago. She wants to videoconference at 1:00 p.m. And she'd like us both to be in on the chat."

To Cady's relief, Jeb was happy to help her out. "Relax," he said as the two of them walked inside the ranch house. "I'm sure it will be fine."

Cady nodded, still trying to convince herself. "I'm sure you're right. It's no big deal." *And even if it is, with you by my side, we'll handle it.*

Cady got her laptop out of her briefcase. They set it up on the screened in back porch, in plain view of the bouncy castle, where the boys were still romping happily.

Short minutes later, they were connected via video to the Stork Agency.

The counselor said hello to them, then Tina stepped into view and pulled up a chair.

It had been a little over a week since Cady had last seen her, but in that time Tina's teenage body had blossomed into full-blown pregnancy. The seventeen-year-old looked tired—as if she wasn't sleeping much—and seemed physically uncomfortable as she tried to settle her bulky form into the straight-backed library chair.

Tina looked at them through her own camera-equipped computer screen. "Hi, Cady. Jeb. I'm really glad you could both talk to me today."

Cady smiled and feigned an inner ease she couldn't begin to feel in this situation. "What's up?" she asked in a tone she hoped would inspire confidence.

Tina bit her lip. "I've been thinking about my dad a lot lately, about how—up until now—he has always been there for me."

Not sure she was following, Cady said cautiously, "And now he's not...because of your pregnancy?"

Tina conceded this was so with a brief dip of her head. "I won't lie to you. It hurts, not having him around. My mom tries to make up for it, but..." She turned tortured eyes to them. "I miss him, you know?"

Cady and Jeb nodded sympathetically. Feeling in

need of some support herself, Cady reached over and took his hand. "Do you think it will be better between you and your dad once the baby is born?" she asked gently.

"I hope so." Tina leaned forward earnestly. "I don't want to go the rest of my life without having a dad there for me. And that started me thinking about baby Zoe...."

Uh-oh, Cady thought, with a sinking feeling in her gut. Here came the inevitable reservation about letting a single mom adopt on her own....

"...and I really want my little girl to have a man in her life when she is growing up. Which is where," Tina said slowly and deliberately, "you come in, Jeb."

"YOU DIDN'T HAVE TO SAY yes so swiftly," Cady told Jeb as soon as the call ended and the computer was shut off.

Surprised by her criticism, he turned to her. "Sure I did."

Cady concentrated on unplugging her computer and putting it back in its case. "Tina and I both would have understood if you'd needed time to think about it."

Jeb could feel her defenses going back up. He drew a calming breath and worked to contain his frustration. "I want to be there for you and baby Zoe, Cady. Tina's suggestion that I do so as Zoe's godfather makes perfect sense. Because Tina is right, every little girl needs both male and female influences in their life."

Cady's slim fingers worried the handle of the case. "What if..." She paused, upset, and shook her head. "What if this exclusive relationship we're having doesn't work out?" With effort, she pivoted to look at him directly. "I know it feels great now, and it is, but in two or five years from now, we might not be so happy. One—or both—of us might grow bored or want to go back to being just friends again. It could get really awkward." She swallowed. "Then what?"

I won't want out, Jeb thought. *And I sure as hell won't ever be bored.*

But sensing that was not what Cady needed to hear at this moment, when she had so little faith in his ability to stick it out for the long haul, Jeb gestured offhandedly instead. "Then we will wish each other well and go on with our lives," he promised, vowing to do whatever he needed to do to gain her trust and faith in him.

In the meantime... "I'll still be Zoe's godfather—and the guy who dotes on her and has since the moment she was born." He caught Cady's hand in his and squeezed companionably. "We'll make it work, and we'll do it because it will be what little Zoe needs."

"THAT WAS SOME princess birthday party you had," Suki told Cady, when her three boys had finished their conversation with their parents and handed the phone back.

"It was." Cady smiled reminiscingly while Jeb took her nephews outside for one last playtime before their baths. "Jeb and the boys went all out. They even gave me a bouncy castle."

Suki laughed. "Sounds like someone sure is sweet on you."

Cady flushed at her older sister's teasing. She still did not want to tempt fate. "Stop it, Suki."

"Okay. I'll let it go for now. So—what did you think of our gift to you?"

Cady gasped. "Can you believe I put it away and forgot to open it?"

"Then do it now," Suki urged. "While we're talking."

Cady went to get it. "Oh Suki…" She stared in wonderment at the beautiful white summer dress and cardigan for her, and the crocheted white layette set and silk-edged blanket for little Zoe.

"I gather you like it?"

Cady clapped a hand over her heart. "It's gorgeous. Thank you, so much!"

"I thought you and the baby both needed a coming-home-from-the-hospital outfit." Her sister's voice was rife with tenderness.

Cady put the lid back on the gift box. "So you approve of what I'm doing?" *Finally?*

"Hermann made me see that it doesn't matter how you come by your family, as long as you have one, and I'm very glad you are getting your own."

"And in a roundabout way, so is Jeb." Briefly, Cady explained about the videoconference with Tina earlier that day.

"Jeb McCabe actually committed to that on the spot? He made a lifelong commitment to the child you're going to adopt?"

"He didn't have to even think about it!" Just as she hadn't had to consider whether or not she wanted them to be exclusive, when he had asked. She had just known that it was the right thing to do, the right thing for her and for him. And now they'd be sharing the experience of adopting a baby. Not in the usual, expected way, but still!

"Hmm." Oblivious to the romantic nature of Cady's

thoughts, Suki continued thoughtfully, "Maybe Jeb McCabe has changed from the guy he was when he left Avalynne Stone at the altar in front of the entire community."

That again. It was all Cady could do not to moan.

Wishing she could explain, knowing she couldn't without breaking her implicit promise to Jeb not to divulge what he had told her, she bit her lip in frustration.

"I'm sorry. I should just let that go," Suki said eventually, when the silence drew out. "Everyone should."

"You're right," Cady said, even more firmly. "They should." The problem was, they wouldn't. Not until something very important changed.

Chapter Eleven

"Do I need to have some bouncers or security guards handy?" Emily McCabe quipped late the following afternoon, after Cady had settled her three nephews in a back booth of the Daybreak Café.

Cady smiled at Jeb's little sister. "No. You don't. And thanks for agreeing to let me have this meeting here, even though your restaurant is technically closed for the day." The bustling eatery served only breakfast and lunch.

"No problem." Emily regarded her with the confidence one would expect from the renowned proprietress and head chef of one of the most popular cafés in the area. "Although I am curious." She waggled her eyebrows and leaned in confidentially. "Does Jeb know you've arranged a meeting with his ex?"

Cady glanced at the three boys, who were coloring happily while waiting for their promised cookies and milk. "No. And I'd prefer you wouldn't say anything."

"Hey." Emily poured two glasses of tea and set a plate of lemon slices on the table. "If you can get Mrs. Stone to cease and desist with all the trash talk she has been spreading about my big brother, I'll help in any way I can."

Cady tensed. "You heard about that?"

"Honey, everyone in town has heard about that. I think that's the reason Avalynne is heading back to Europe a few days ahead of schedule. And speaking of ex-fiancées..." Emily patted Cady's arm. "...here she is."

Jeb's sister gave her an encouraging smile and went back to the booth to sit with the boys.

Cady walked to the front of the restaurant to meet with Avalynne. As soon as they sat down, the stunning auburn-haired artist cut straight to the chase. "I gather this has something to do with Jeb?"

She nodded. "Your mother came to see me the other evening. She went to see Jeb's parents, too."

Avalynne did not seem surprised or particularly upset. She stirred sweetener into her tea, her expression guarded. "I'm sure Jeb told you and his parents that the two of us are just friends," she stated.

Cady held out hope that Avalynne would finally see the light and do the right thing. "Unfortunately, I don't think your mother believes that—and her doubt has spread to Jeb's parents."

The other woman sipped her tea. "If you know anything about my mom, you know I don't have any sway over her. She does what she wants. And my father always backs her up."

So as far as Avalynne was concerned, trying to deal with her parents was a lost cause. But while Cady understood you couldn't change someone who didn't want to change, there was a larger issue at stake. She tried again to get Avalynne to see the light. "All this talk is not fair to Jeb. It's dredging up the past."

"I'm sure he can handle it." Avalynne gulped the rest

of her iced tea and stood. "Now if you'll excuse me, I've got a plane to catch." She slung her bag over her shoulder and walked out the door.

So much for her plan to subtly bring out the truth and clear Jeb's reputation once and for all, Cady thought.

Emily returned to her side. "That didn't go well."

She grimaced, wishing otherwise. "No. It didn't."

The chef shook her head in consternation. "For the life of me, I can't figure out why Avalynne and Jeb are still friends."

Because Jeb is a good guy and he wants to protect those he senses need protecting.

Emily brought another glass to the table and poured some iced tea for herself. "I get why Jeb is nice to her—he has all that guilt about what he did, leaving her at the altar. But why she would forgive him to the point she has—when she is clearly not in love with him—is beyond me. It's almost as if she's sort of…dependent on him in some way."

Heck yes, Avalynne was dependent on Jeb, Cady thought sourly. The adventuress needed Jeb to keep her secrets from her family.

Emily peered at her speculatively. "But I can see you care about him, Cady."

She gazed back at Jeb's little sister. "I do," she admitted honestly. *In fact, I may very well be falling in love with him. Not that I dare disclose that, either.*

Concern glimmered in Emily's eyes. "Be careful."

Cady guessed where this was going, but Emily's assumption was based on a falsehood. "He's not going to break my heart," she assured her resolutely. That much she knew.

Emily sighed and looked out the window, in the

direction Avalynne had gone. "That," she said sorrow-fully, "is what all the women who fall in Jeb's path say."

"You were busy today," Jeb said, later that evening after the kids were asleep.

Cady flushed guiltily. She had only to look into his eyes to realize he knew what she had been up to while in town that afternoon.

She turned the oven knob to 350 and headed for the walk-in pantry. "How'd you hear about my meeting with Avalynne?"

Jeb watched her get out the flour, sugar, baking powder and salt and carry them back to the work island. "A couple of ways. Emily called, fishing for information. Avalynne texted, too."

Cady felt a little twinge of jealousy despite herself. She reached into the cupboard and pulled out a baking pan and two stainless steel mixing bowls. "And?"

Jeb leaned against the counter. "She apologized for her mother's behavior and suggested I talk to my folks again and clear up any misunderstanding."

Cady paused to look at him. "Did you do that?"

The features of his face set grimly. "No. It wouldn't do any good. They're going to believe what they believe."

Cady measured dry ingredients into a bowl, glad she had a task to occupy her. "You sound like Avalynne now...."

He shrugged. "I guess that's something my ex and I have in common."

Silence fell as Cady creamed the softened butter and sugar, then mixed in egg, milk and vanilla.

Jeb looked at her as if he wanted to do a lot more

than stand there and talk. "Do you want to know what else Avalynne texted?"

Cady wanted to do a lot more than stand there and talk, too.

"I don't know." She made a comical face. Figuring as long as Jeb was there, he might as well make himself useful, she handed him a stack of paper baking liners and the muffin tin. "Do I?"

He lifted a brow. "She wanted to know if I was hooking up with you."

Cady blushed and ignored the thrill rushing through her. Her need to protect her privacy warred with her equally strong wish to tell the world. She studied the inscrutable look on Jeb's handsome face and swallowed self-consciously. "Why would she think that?"

Finished with his task, he edged even closer. "She thought you seemed very protective of me."

Aware that their shoulders were nearly touching, Cady concentrated on folding the dry ingredients into the wet. "I was just looking out for you."

The oven dinged, signaling it was preheated.

Jeb's gaze narrowed. "Because of our bet?"

And because I adore you. And want only the best for you. Leery of saying anything that sounded too cheesy, however, Cady shrugged. "I know you encouraged me to forget about our wager, but it doesn't seem right, given the fact you've so clearly won." She paused to look into his eyes, then, leery of the feelings welling up inside her, rushed on. "You do have what it takes to go the distance with the kids. And in fact, have helped me greatly, when it comes to caring for them and calming them down. I've gained a lot of confidence, thanks to you."

Jeb's eyes lit with pleasure. He tucked the curtain of

hair behind her ear. "So in return, you're going to use your considerable brain power to figure out a way for me to put the scandal with Avalynne in the past where it belongs."

Cady folded chunks of fresh peaches into the batter. "It'd be easy to do if I could just tell the truth about what really happened that day."

His smile faded and he moved away. "I told you— I'm not going to do that. It would cause way too much drama."

And personal drama was something the easygoing Jeb hated.

Cady scooped batter into the cups and slid the pan into the oven. She set the timer, then turned back to him.

Caring enough to risk irritating him further, she approached him once again. "The only problem is I'm not sure I can succeed in freeing you from the past without that."

Their eyes meshed.

She took his hand in hers and went on, "Because it seems like you're right—people won't ever forget about what happened with you and Avalynne without knowing the real story."

Even Emily had brought up the ignominious tale. Although Cady had no intention of telling Jeb that. He'd been hurt enough by the continuing gossip.

Jeb's free hand covered their entwined fingers. "You're probably right," he said, squeezing gently. "The destructive talk won't end until my present is a lot more interesting than my past."

Cady didn't trust the sudden glitter in his eyes. She tensed. "What did you have in mind?"

"Simple." He brought her hand to his lips and kissed it. "I let everyone see me with someone else." He wrapped his arms around her waist and tugged her closer. "We go public with our romance and let everyone know we are now exclusive."

Our romance. Cady's heartbeat quickened as she splayed her hands across the hard muscles of his chest. "Are you sure you want to do that?" She contemplated the implications. "It would cause a lot of talk. And put a lot of extra pressure on us, too." Plus, ill-conceived dalliances could easily crash and burn, when put too harshly to the test. She certainly didn't want to risk that!

Jeb rubbed his thumb over her cheek. He wasn't worried. "Or doing so might make us even happier and help us succeed as a couple."

"Jeb..."

He backed her up against the wall and caged her with his arms. "This feels right, Cady. That's all we need to think about...."

What felt right in the moment was all Jeb ever seemed to consider. Yet as he lowered his head and kissed her, being with him like this was suddenly all Cady wanted to consider, too.

He made her feel so desirable and so wanted. And he made her feel cherished, too, and foolish or not, she was not willing to give that up.

"GOT A MINUTE?" Jeb's brother Hank asked, at four-thirty the next afternoon.

Jeb ushered him into the house. "Sure. If you don't mind coming back to the kitchen. It's my turn to make dinner."

"Wow," Hank remarked as they strolled into Suki and Hermann's elegantly appointed kitchen. He breathed in the aromatic scents of garlic, browning beef and tomato sauce. "The rumors about your domestication seem to be true."

Jeb adjusted the flame beneath the sizzling meatballs. He made no apology for his culinary skill. "You're one to talk. You've been nothing but a homebody since you married Ally."

He beamed. "What can I say? She makes me happy."

Jeb could see that.

"Where is Cady?"

Jeb emptied a box of spaghetti into the pot of boiling water. "Out back, supervising the kids on their swing set."

Hank looked out the window over the sink, to the backyard. He smiled at the boisterous activity going on. "Ah, yes. So, are you and Cady getting as serious about each other as our baby sister seems to think?"

Jeb knew the once untamable Emily had been incredibly romantic since she'd married Dylan Reeves. To the point she was seeing and feeling love everywhere.

But...*serious?* Jeb knew how he felt, and had for some time, but he also knew there was a big difference between the infatuation of a new fling and actually being in love with someone. It didn't mean you couldn't get there. But it didn't necessarily mean that you would, either.

So he called on what he and Cady had agreed their public stance on their relationship would be, and stuck to that. "We're romantically involved—exclusively."

His brother ambled closer and helped himself to one

of the croutons Jeb had set out for the salad. "That's all?" He looked disappointed.

Jeb avoided answering the question directly. "I prefer to play my cards close to my chest." He didn't want to jinx it. Things were going so well….

Hank nodded, understanding the need for privacy. "Fair enough."

The back door opened and Cady walked in. She smiled at Hank in surprise. "Hey, stranger." She gave Jeb's brother a one-armed hug and a kiss on the cheek. "I didn't know you were here."

Hank hugged and kissed her back. "I came over to talk business with Jeb."

"Well, don't let me stop you," she said merrily. "I just came in to get some Popsicles for the boys."

She went to the freezer.

Hank turned back to Jeb. "I heard you were passing on the black baldie bull you looked at over in King County."

Jeb went back to stirring the meatballs sizzling in the skillet. "That's true."

The two of them continued talking as Cady went back out, frozen treats in hand. When she returned to throw away the sticks ten minutes later, Hank had already departed. "Everything okay?" she asked Jeb.

That probably would depend on who you asked, he thought with no small trace of irony.

Casually, he brought Cady up to date. "Hank was trying to convince me to purchase the bull."

Suddenly, her mood became as cautious as his brother's. "Why aren't you?" she came closer, wanting to understand. "Is there something wrong with it?"

"On the contrary," Jeb said, with no small trace of regret. "It would be a great stud. The best I've seen."

Cady narrowed her eyes in confusion. "Then?"

Jeb grimaced. "It's too much of a financial commitment at the outset. I can use artificial insemination and embryo transfers to multiply the offspring from my herd for a lot less money."

Seeming to understand he needed a sounding board, she put her hands into the pockets of her shorts and slipped into business mode. "In the short run, I can see why that would be advisable. What about the long run?"

Jeb turned his glance away from her sleek, sexy legs and slim feet. "I don't know that I'll want to be in the cattle breeding business for more than a few years."

He expected Cady to understand that, as she did most everything about him. Instead, she went very still.

He emptied the cooked pasta into the strainer in the sink. Fragrant steam scented the air. "A lot of things could happen." *I could decide I wanted to live closer to Houston. Or maybe in Houston.* "I don't even know if I'll still have this ranch." Jeb transferred the cooked spaghetti to the serving dish. He carried the platter to the stove, added sauce and meatballs.

Her expression thoughtful—and suddenly, maddeningly inscrutable—Cady handed him the wedge of Parmesan cheese and the grater. "You could be on to something new and different and exciting?" she summed up, as if that would be the most natural occurrence in the world.

"Change can be good." Jeb added a sprinkling of cheese then looked over at her. "Especially the unexpected kind."

Cady nodded again, a distant look in her eyes. "Well, good luck with your new breeding operation," she murmured. "I'm sure whatever decision you make will be the right one for you."

Without another word, she opened the door and called the boys to come in for dinner.

"YOU SOUND DOWN TONIGHT," Suki noted, hours later.

Cady snuggled in the covers of her bed, her cell phone pressed to her ear. She had told Jeb she had some work email to catch up on—which was true—and turned in early…alone. He'd looked puzzled, but she had known she needed time to process everything that had happened in the last week. "I think I'm just tired," she fibbed now.

Suki sympathized. "No doubt the boys have worn you out."

It wasn't that, Cady knew, so much as her renewed worry over the way she was recklessly risking her heart to a man who didn't seem to know the first thing about long-term commitment to anything. Except maybe the necessity of frequent change. But not wanting to get into that with her protective older sister, she just said, "You're probably right."

"Then you're really going to be happy with what I have to tell you right now," Suki said, sounding remarkably joyous herself.

Cady furrowed her brow in confusion. "And what is that?" she asked drily, wondering what Suki was up to now.

"Go downstairs and open the front door, and see for yourself," she ordered.

Surely not another birthday gift! "Are you serious?"

"As the rain in July. Seriously, Cady," Suki insisted, even more firmly, *"do as I ask!"*

With a sigh, Cady got out of bed, found her slippers and her robe, and headed down the stairs.

"What's up?" Jeb asked, from the living room sofa, as she passed by.

Aware he had never looked more sexy and relaxed than he did at that moment, Cady shrugged. "I'm about to find out."

Smiling, Jeb got up to join her, and they walked together toward the front door.

Chapter Twelve

"Momma! Daddy!" the boys cried jubilantly, when they entered the kitchen early the next morning and found Cady and their parents gathered around the table. "You're home!"

Suki and Hermann grinned at the warm welcome and took their three offspring into their arms. "We missed you all so much we finished up our work early and got in late last night!" the jet-lagged Suki told them.

With furrowed brow, Dalton asked, "Where's Our Friend Jeb? He's not in his bed."

"He went back to his ranch last night and slept there," Cady explained.

And while she knew it was the logical thing to do, she still felt bereft. It may have been foolish, but she had gotten used to seeing him first thing in the morning, and the last thing at night.

"But we want him to stay here!" Finn pouted. "We want you both to stay here with us, Aunt Cady!"

Micah climbed out of his mother's arms and onto Cady's lap. He wrapped his arms around her neck. "Stay here," he commanded.

"Oh, honey, I wish I could," Cady said, rubbing the

two-year-old's back. "But I've got to get to Houston. I have a lot of stuff to get caught up on there."

That was an understatement. She had a nursery mural to decide on, a baby to help usher into the world, adoption proceedings to get through, a maternity schedule to arrange, babysitters to find…. The list went on and on.

Plus, it was time to get back to her real life, Cady told herself firmly, and relinquish the fantasy she'd been living for the past couple weeks.

"We understand." Suki smiled as she poured all the adults more coffee.

Hermann nodded. "We can't thank you enough. Jeb, too."

Cady had some gratitude of her own to express, so on her way out of Laramie County, she stopped by Jeb's ranch.

She saw him out in a field, standing amid the crop of new black baldie calves and their mamas, pumping fresh water into the troughs. Her heart beating quickly, she walked out to join him. He looked good in the morning sunshine, his straw hat drawn low across his brow. Wondering if he had missed her last night as much as she had missed him, Cady couldn't help admiring how his chambray shirt clung to the solid muscles of his chest and shoulders, the way the worn jeans gloved his rock hard thighs.

"Hi."

A bleating calf brushed up against Jeb's leg. He directed it toward its mother, then smiled back. His glance sifted over Cady's tailored slacks and sleeveless linen blouse. "Headed back to Houston?"

Cady wished that wasn't the case. If only she could stay here indefinitely… "It's time."

He nodded in understanding, an inscrutable expression in his eyes. "I figured as much." He went back to pumping water, the muscles in his back and shoulders straining against the fabric of his shirt.

Cady edged closer still, being careful where she stepped. "I want to thank you for all you did for us. The boys and I wouldn't have made it if you hadn't helped out."

He offered an aimless shrug. "Sure you would have. It just would have been a lot louder and more chaotic, but you would have figured out a way to survive the uproar." When the troughs were full of fresh water for the brood cows and their calves, he turned back to her, his expression confident. "You always do."

She lifted a hand to shade her eyes from the summer sun. "I think you're giving me a lot more credit than I'm due."

"Or vice versa." Jeb touched her shoulder gently, turning her toward the pasture gate. Together, they walked through the field. He let her exit first, then followed, shutting the gate behind them. "Maybe the point is we make a good team." He steered her to the shade of a nearby tree. "What happened last night, anyway?"

Cady settled against the rough bark of the live oak. "What do you mean?"

He tipped up the brim of his hat. "You were upset with me."

Guilt mixed with embarrassment. "I was tired."

"No," Jeb corrected, deadpan. "You were disappointed I wasn't going to buy that bull. And for the life of me I can't figure out why. Unless…you're against artificial insemination by strangers for bulls, as well as humans…?"

Cady couldn't help it—she laughed at the notion. "Believe me, it has nothing to do with that," she said, echoing his droll tone.

Jeb sobered. "Then what *does* it have to do with?"

Your inability to commit to anything or anyone long-term, or so it would seem. Unable to say that, however, without coming across as judgmental, she sidestepped the issue and said as honestly as possible, "The whole conversation just reminded me that you and I lead very separate lives. You're here… I'm in Houston."

He frowned in obvious confusion. "The distance has never stopped us from seeing each other before."

Cady drew in a jerky breath. "I know." Wary of revealing too much, she moved around him and headed toward her car.

"But now it's different." Once again, Jeb fell into step beside her.

The heels of her sandals clicked as she reached the paved drive. "It shouldn't be. I know." She increased her pace to her car and grabbed for the handle on the driver's door. "That was the agreement."

He stopped her, a hand to her wrist. "Then maybe it's time you and I came up with a new agreement," he told her solemnly.

Cady caught her breath and looked up into the smoky depths of his eyes.

"I want us to be lovers, Cady," he told her softly, tenderly encircling her wrist. "I don't care if it is long distance. As long as we find a way to keep building on everything we have enjoyed this week."

JEB HADN'T MEANT to blurt out the words or proposition Cady that way. Knowing how skittish she was, he had intended to slowly work up to taking the next big step in their relationship.

But as he had feared, instead of welcoming the suggestion with all her heart, Cady hesitated.

Her eyes were as troubled as her low voice as she said, "Like you told me, we don't have to decide anything right now."

The problem was, Jeb *wanted* to wrest some sort of promise of a future together from her right now. He was sure, deep down, that was what she wanted, too. If only he could get her to admit it.

Cady reached in through the open car window and got her phone. She sighed, seeing the 2 Missed Calls message on her screen, and diverted her attention to that. "Hang on a minute. I've got to…oh my goodness, Jeb! The Stork Agency has been trying to get hold of me!"

She punched in another command and put the phone to her ear. As she listened to the messages left on her voice mail, her face turned pink, then white, then pink again.

Cady's jaw dropped. "They're taking Tina Matthews to the hospital. She's in labor!"

She punched in the number with trembling fingers, heard the error chimes, then did it again, slower and more carefully this time. Her eyes still locked with Jeb's, she exhaled in relief as the call finally went through. "Hi. It's Cady. Yes, I'll be there. Unfortunately, I'm about four hours away." She paused. "I'll see if he can be there, too. Yes." She smiled. "See you soon."

Cady ended the call and gazed into Jeb's eyes. "I know it's a lot to ask…"

"Hey." Jeb angled his thumb at the center of his chest. "I'm Zoe's godfather." *And the man who wants to have you and your baby in my life forever.* "Of course I'll be there, too."

CADY WAITED FOR JEB to throw some things in a bag, and then she led the way in her car. He followed in his pickup truck. Which was good, since they didn't have to talk further about his proposition, when she felt incapable of doing so. And bad, because she really could have used him right by her side during the 232 mile trek.

Once at their destination, they parked in the garage, met up in the center aisle and walked toward the hospital entrance. As if sensing how much she needed him, he reached over and took her hand.

Cady reveled in the warmth and strength of his grasp.

"Nervous?" He leaned down to whisper in her ear.

She whispered back, "My knees are wobbling."

He let go of her hand and pulled her into the reassuring curve of his body. His arm tightened around her shoulders and he bent to press a kiss in her hair. "It's going to be okay."

When he said it like that, she could almost believe him. Cady drew a bolstering breath and pushed her mounting anxiety aside. All she wanted to feel right now was excitement. "You'd think I was the one having the baby!" she complained.

Jeb winked. "In a way, we both are."

Cady smiled at the thought of Jeb being little Zoe's godfather, and she, little Zoe's mom.

She reached in her purse and put her hand on the

ultrasound photo she had brought with her. Maybe it was silly, but knowing she had it reassured her.

Together, she and Jeb stepped through the automatic glass doors.

Minutes later, they were walking up to the desk in the maternity wing.

"I'm here to see Tina Matthews," Cady said.

The nurse pointed to their left. "She went thataway."

Cady and Jeb looked down the corridor. Sure enough, the pregnant teen was walking down the hall, in a hospital gown, robe and slippers. She had one hand pressed to the middle of her back, another to her tummy. With her were two people Cady had never seen before. But she could guess who they were by the striking familial resemblance, when they turned and headed back Jeb and Cady's way.

Seeing them standing there, Tina broke into a wide smile. She lifted her hand in an enthusiastic wave. "Come and meet my folks! Mom and Dad, I want you to meet Cady Keilor. She's going to adopt Zoe. And this is Jeb McCabe—he's going to be her godfather."

Hands were shaken. Hellos said.

"I'm surprised to see you on your feet," Cady said, happy that she had apparently made up with her parents.

Tina rolled her eyes at her current predicament. "They're hoping walking will speed up my labor."

"As slow as it's going," Mrs. Matthews said, "they think it could be up to twenty-four hours before she actually delivers. Maybe even more."

Tina groaned. "Mom. Please. Don't say that. I don't think I can do this for that long."

A kind-faced nurse joined them. "It's a first baby,

Tina, honey. And first babies are known for being slow."
The nurse turned to Cady and Jeb. "We're only going
to allow two people in the delivery room with her."

Tina looked at Cady with a mixture of urgency
and apology. "And I want it to be my mom and dad.
Okay?"

"YOU'RE TAKING THIS awfully well," Jeb said as the
two of them left the hospital, only a few minutes after
they had arrived.

Cady paused beside her car and lifted her hands in a
helpless manner. "What could I say? If I were in Tina's
place, I'd want my parents at my side, too. Besides, the
nurse said she'd call me when the time was near, so I
could be on the premises for the big event."

"In the meantime, it looks like we have some time
to kill," Jeb said.

No joke. Twenty-four hours loomed ahead of them
like an abyss. Cady sighed. "What do you want to
do?"

He put his hands on her shoulders. "Go on a date."

Ignoring the comforting warmth of his palms, Cady
echoed, "A date?"

Jeb winked and leaned in close. "You know. The thing
where a guy and a gal get dressed up and go out together
and do something fun. Like dinner and a movie…"

Cady fought the unexpected thrill coursing through
her, and backed up against the car door. "I know you
mean well, but…I'm not sure I could concentrate enough
to be decent company."

Jeb dropped his hands to his sides. "Then what would
you like to do?" he asked gently.

She could feel his body heat, and breathed in the

enticing scent of his masculine cologne. "Go back to my place."

His gaze lingering on her lips, he flashed a tantalizing half smile. "With or without me?"

Cady struggled to get a handle on the need welling up inside her. Like the fact that she no longer wanted to adopt this baby completely on her own, but wanted Jeb involved, too, as the steady male presence in the child's life. And maybe—if she was completely honest—hers, too...

She swallowed. "What do you think?"

They barely made it in the front door to her loft when Jeb put his bag down and swung Cady off her feet.

She luxuriated in the feeling of being held against his broad chest. With her heart aflutter and her libido in overdrive, she teased, "If this is about me owing you an entire night in your arms..."

He carried her to her bed and set her down beside it. "I think it's about us owing *each other* an entire night in one another's arms."

Cady couldn't say she didn't want that, too. Making hot, passionate love with Jeb was the best way she knew to forget everything that was worrying her.

She wound her arms around his shoulders and offered her lips up to his. "Then let's go for it," she said.

The first touch of their lips was electric, hot, enticing. His hands moved down the small of her back, his tongue swept inside her mouth and she tasted the male essence of him. She arched against him, enjoying the long, delicious kisses, the feeling of being what he wanted and needed, too.

Still kissing her, he unbuttoned her blouse and drew it off, unfastened the clasp on her bra. Cool air assaulted her skin. Seconds later, the warmth of his callused palms moved slowly, lovingly upward, over her ribs. Her nipples heated and swelled as he cupped her breasts. The tingling deepened with the suction of his mouth, and so did her yearning to have him inside her.

Cady moaned and felt her knees go weak.

Aware she had never felt as soft and womanly as she did with him, she unclasped his belt buckle and lowered the zipper on his jeans. Touched him until his body throbbed and demanded more. All the while she was wishing she could tell him he was the one for her, and always would be. That she wanted them to be more than lovers, or friends, or loving attendants to the baby she was soon to adopt.

She wanted Jeb to love her as much as she now knew she loved him. In that all-or-nothing, we-have-to-be-married-to-be-truly-happy way. But realizing those words carried the weight of an emotional commitment Jeb might not ever be ready to make, she concentrated on what they were able to bring to each other instead.

Friendship. Understanding. A feeling of being loved and appreciated, even if the actual words were never said. And physical fireworks unlike any she had ever dreamed existed.

And now, with the baby she had wanted forever just hours from being born, her own family ready to be made, Cady knew her life was finally on the brink of being complete.

JEB DIDN'T KNOW what he had done to deserve a woman like Cady. He didn't care. All he knew was that in the course of the last ten days, everything had changed. He and Cady had gone from being friends to lovers. And though she had yet to promise him she would be his woman from here on out, the way she surrendered to his kisses told him everything he needed to know.

He could no longer imagine his life without her in it, and as her hands swept over his body, molding and exploring, he suspected she felt the same.

Together, they finished undressing and eased down onto the bed, the wildness in Cady matching the untamed part of him. He moved onto his back and pulled her on top of him, kissing her all the while. Then rolled, so they were on their sides. And again, so she was beneath him, her legs spread wide.

"Now," she whispered.

"Not so fast," he told her, sliding lower.

She laughed quietly, then moaned as his lips made a detour around and over her breasts. She threaded her hands through his hair and caught his head as he worked the nipples into tender points of desire. "Jeb..."

Enjoying the erratic rhythm of her breath and the trembling of her limbs, he caressed the insides of her thighs, the gentle slope of her ribs and the nip of her waist. "I know you want me," he whispered back, "but I want to take our time...."

Her spine arched as he dipped his tongue into her navel, and she whimpered again, this time in acquiescence.

Pleased at her response, he went lower still, enjoying the delicate floral fragrance of her perfume, the silky warmth of her skin. Loving the way she yielded to him, he brought her nearer and found the sweet perfection. Held her as she went over the edge. Then moved upward again.

Love filled her eyes as he eased her back against

the pillows and settled between her legs. Their lips met again. He drew her flush against him, pouring everything he felt, everything he had ever needed and wanted, into the kiss. Her body heated, as did his. She rose up to meet him. He lifted her hips and plunged deep, sliding all the way home, their bodies taking up the rhythm of tender acceptance and driving need.

Again and again he loved her, knowing he wanted her as he had never wanted anyone before. And only when he was sure she knew how important they were to each other, and always would be, did he let the rightness of the moment draw them all the way in, propelling them into ecstasy and beyond.

Chapter Thirteen

The phone rang at 4:45 A.M. Cady awoke with a start and extricated herself from Jeb's arms. Shaking her head to clear the cobwebs, she mumbled a sleepy hello. Listened intently and then, with a mixture of anticipation and excitement filling her heart, said, "I—we—will be right there. Thanks so much for calling."

Jeb lifted an eyebrow as she put the receiver back in the charger. "Tina?"

Thrilling at the way he looked, lounging naked in her bed, Cady related, "The nurse predicts that Tina will deliver Zoe in the next hour."

With a smile creasing his handsome face, Jeb threw the covers back, displaying even more of his masculine form. "Let's go."

Bubbling with joy, Cady hurried to get ready, too. In ten minutes, they were out the front door. Thirty minutes after that, they were at the hospital, anxiously pacing the maternity ward lounge with the other extended families, awaiting word.

Finally, at shortly after seven, the nurse appeared. She had the relaxed, genial body language of someone who had assisted in a birth where all had gone well.

"Cady Keilor? Jeb McCabe? Tina Matthews and baby Zoe are ready to see you now."

Cady's heart pounded. With a smile on his face, Jeb took her hand, engulfing it in his warm grasp.

The nurse led them back to the birthing room.

As they entered, Mr. and Mrs. Matthews departed. Cady noted the teen's parents did not make eye contact with her or Jeb. She tried not to make too much of it as she neared Tina's bedside. This must be hard on them, she thought, losing their first biological grandchild to adoption.

The seventeen-year-old looked remarkably composed, and as she turned her glance to Cady, she looked sad, too. But not for herself.

Cady's heart began to sink.

Cradling her sleeping infant protectively to her chest, Tina swallowed. Her face was pale, her gaze determined. And Cady knew in an instant the news was not good.

"The counselor from the Stork Agency said I didn't have to talk to you if I didn't want to, but I told her that I wanted to explain to you myself…."

Disappointment roared through Cady as she interjected, "That you've decided to keep your baby?"

Tears trembled on Tina's lashes. "I'm so sorry to disappoint you," she said, with obvious regret, "but everything is different now. My parents aren't mad at me anymore. They want me to keep Zoe, and they said they'd help me. I've given this a lot of thought…and I know it's the right thing to do."

Cady pulled up a chair beside the bed. Her heart broke as she smiled at the teenager. "I understand," she said softly, forcing herself to rise above her own selfish concerns and think about what was best for everyone in this situation. And that started with being painfully honest.

"If I were in your place…" Cady felt herself begin to tear up, too. Determinedly, she blinked back the moisture and swallowed around the lump in her throat. "I'd want to keep my baby." Out of the corner of her eye, she saw Jeb, his jaw so taut his cheek muscles could have been carved in stone.

"The agency said they would reimburse all your fees," Tina continued. "My mom and dad are going to pay them."

The money was the least of Cady's concern. "Sounds like everything is settled, then." Feeling numb and bereft, she stood.

In addition to losing the baby, she had lost part of her future connection to Jeb.

All at once, Cady felt the happiness—the hope—of the last few weeks slipping away.

Tina searched her eyes, not about to change her mind, but obviously wondering how to help. "Did you want to hold Zoe before you leave?" she asked softly.

Cady looked down at the sweetly sleeping infant who had once been a cherished part of her and Jeb's future. "Yes." She held out her arms, for an even more moving goodbye. "I would."

JEB HAD NEVER CONSIDERED himself a particularly emotional person, but seeing Cady take the infant into her arms and hold her tenderly against her chest damn near broke his heart. The poignant scene made him want to burst into tears.

"She's beautiful," Cady whispered, giving the tiny

infant one long last, loving look. "And very much like you…"

"Thank you," Tina murmured, overcome with joy. She looked at Jeb. "Do you want to hold her, too?"

The funny thing was, he did.

Not trusting himself to speak, he nodded.

Cady gently made the transfer to his arms.

It wasn't the first time Jeb had held a newborn infant. But it was the first time cradling one felt like an arrow to his heart.

He hadn't realized until now how much he had wanted a baby in his life. How much he wanted to share this experience with Cady. Her grace and unyielding empathy in this heart-rending situation only proved how much love and understanding she had to give, not to just her own child, but to all those around her.

Aware that he had never respected Cady more, he handed the newborn infant back to her momma. "Zoe is one sweet baby," he told Tina gruffly.

Tears misting her eyes, Cady murmured, "We wish you all the happiness in the world."

"Thank you," Tina whispered back, as she cuddled her baby once again.

Jeb and Cady slipped out.

Tina's parents were waiting anxiously in the hall. They glanced at Cady and Jeb. There wasn't much for anyone to say; the situation was what it was. Nods of mutual empathy and understanding were exchanged. Tina's parents looked relieved that there was to be no ugly scene or recriminations.

Wordlessly, Cady and Jeb continued on down the hall. He took her hand in the elevator.

She clasped his tightly and kept gripping it all the way to his pickup truck.

Jeb had an idea how much Cady was hurting, how difficult it was for her to keep it together. Figuring the least he could give her was the space she apparently needed, he asked quietly, "Where to?"

She looked out the window, her composure intact, her demeanor more distant than he had ever seen it. "Home, please."

Jeb turned on the stereo. The soothing sounds of Alan Jackson's voice accompanied them on the drive.

Cady still looked as numb as Jeb felt as they took the elevator to her loft.

She walked inside, dropped her bag on the table.

Spread out on the coffee table were the going home from the hospital outfits her sister and brother-in-law had given her. Next to that, the ultrasound photo of Zoe, taken a week before she was born.

Cady stood, looking down at it all.

Jeb expected her to burst into tears, to let loose the flood of disappointment that had to be welling up inside her. Instead, he got…nothing.

Wishing like hell he could comfort her, he came up behind her. He placed gentle hands on her shoulders, wishing he knew how to reach her. "You can cry, you know," he told her softly.

And I'll cry right along with you….

Cady exhaled and shook her head in mute refusal. Her sadness palpable, she paced away from him to the windows overlooking the city of Houston. "You want to know what's ironic about all this?"

Jeb nodded and took up a place opposite her.

Cady swallowed. "It's that all along, I had a feeling

in my gut that this adoption would be like everything else in my personal life I've ever wanted to work out."

Her expression unbearably sad, she ran a finger down the metal frame edging the big panes of glass. Sighed again, then shook her head. "All those guys I brought home to meet the family, who promptly fell in love with my gorgeous older sister."

Grimacing, she continued her recitation. "The other birth moms who chose anyone else but me to adopt their baby. And now..."

Moisture glimmered in her eyes.

"...when I was finally selected to be the adoptive mom..." she lifted her hands in disappointment "this..."

In all the time he had known her, Jeb had never seen Cady give up on anything she really wanted to achieve—until now. Aware she was about to throw in the towel on ever having a family, he counseled gently, "This doesn't have to be the end of the road, Cady."

She turned a disillusioned glance to his.

Jeb swallowed, aware he was about to make the kind of long-term commitment he'd never considered. And it was all because of Cady—because she had made him see there was more to life than just living with your humor intact and your guard up.

He edged close enough to inhale the lingering scent of her perfume. He touched the silky soft skin of her face. "There's no physical reason you can't have a baby on your own, a baby no one can take from you."

Cady stepped back, resentment edging her low tone. "I've told you how I feel about artificial insemination."

He could see she expected him to argue the point with

her. Instead, he informed her calmly, "But you haven't told me how you feel about having a baby with me."

Silence fell as his words sank in.

Cady blinked in stunned amazement. "What are you talking about?"

What he hadn't admitted to himself he could ever want again—until now.

Jeb drew a breath and looked her straight in the eye. "I'm talking about marriage. Between you and me."

Cady inhaled sharply, all the color leaving her face, then returning in a riotous bloom of pink. She gasped again. "Jeb!"

He didn't have to be a rocket scientist to see she was about to turn him down, right out of the gate.

Squaring his shoulders, he took her hand and determinedly listed the reasons why they should forgo convention and head down this road. "We've been friends for years. We know each other intimately. Sexually, we're definitely on the same page. And we get along great. Plus we both want kids."

Cady wrested her hand from his as if he had burned her. "Since when?" she demanded, with a stubborn tilt to her chin.

Jeb frowned, upset by her wariness. "Since I spent the last week with you and the boys, and agreed to be godfather to the baby you were hoping to adopt!"

Her expression gentled slightly.

Encouraged, Jeb continued, a lot less defensively, "I've never seen a future for myself that felt really right, Cady." He took her hand again, tenderly this time. "But this one does."

She stared down at their entwined fingers. Thinking, deliberating. "For now," she murmured, the disillusionment edging back into her low tone. She shifted her glance and looked up at him. "What happens when time passes and you decide marriage to me, and kids, isn't for you, after all?"

Okay. He was getting a little tired of being the suspect in all this. Cady knew he was one hell of a lot more gallant than his reputation, when it came to women.

Still, she had been through a lot, so he tried to rein in his hurt feelings and be patient. Still facing her, he braced a shoulder against the window and folded his arms in front of him. "What are you talking about?"

Cady shrugged, acting as if they had never really known each other at all. Or held each other through the night...

"Your history of falling into things because they're convenient and seem to make you happy at the time," she told him remotely.

She crossed her arms beneath her breasts. "It's why you started doing rodeo. Why you bought your ranch and began boarding rodeo stock, and why you're now contemplating getting rid of that business and going full time into breeding black baldie cattle."

So he'd never settled down professionally, the way she had. So he liked to try out different ways of making a living, instead of being focused on one area, such as marketing. So what?

He grimaced. "That's different."

Cady lifted an eyebrow, all cool elegance now. "I wish it were," she said quietly.

Moving away from him, she went back to the coffee table, picked up the ultrasound photo and the gifts, and shoved them in a drawer.

The offending items out of sight, she turned back to

him, her countenance resolute. "But if we don't want to get hurt again, we have to be honest here. We never would have been together this last week if you hadn't been teasing me and we hadn't made that stupid bet," she told him with a practicality that stung. "We never would have made love, or gotten temporarily close."

"Temporarily?" Jeb echoed unhappily. Was this all their time together had meant to her?

CADY BEGAN TO PACE, her long sexy legs catching his eye as she roamed from one side of her loft to the other. "I know this seems like the perfect solution to all our problems," she told him. "We marry and I get the baby I want, the old-fashioned way."

"The baby we both want," Jeb corrected.

She nodded, accepting that. "And in the process, you shock people so much they'd finally stop talking about your inability to commit long-term to Avalynne Stone... and they'd begin talking about how you fell hard enough to marry and have a baby with me."

That was a low blow, Jeb thought.

"You'd finally get back your reputation as a stand-up guy," she continued, oblivious to his mounting anger and dismay. "Which would definitely make your family very happy." She sighed. "And Suki and Hermann and the boys would be over the moon if I had a family of my own, too."

"That's not the reason I am proposing this!" Jeb interrupted, with a building resentment of his own.

Once again she did not believe him.

She came closer, her hands outstretched, her expression compassionate. "Jeb, I know how gallant you are at heart," she told him, with a patience he'd neither asked for nor needed.

He glared at her, too peeved to scrounge up an appropriate comeback.

"I know you want to rescue me and somehow make this all better." She backed up. "But pretending we love each other enough to make a marriage work for the rest of our lives is not the way."

Cady's soft lips took on that stubborn pout he knew so well.

"And I'll be damned if I ever pledge my heart in a stopgap way, only to end up facing divorce a few years down the road," she finished firmly.

Jeb had heard a variation of this same speech years ago.

"Face it, Jeb," Avalynne had said. "We don't love each other and never will. We have to end this here and now if we ever want a chance to be happy…."

Only now it was Cady standing here, saying the same thing, asking for the same release.

Feeling as if his whole life had just been blown to smithereens, Jeb forced her to spell it out. "So you're saying…?"

"Whatever this has been between us, is over," she replied in a flat, irrevocable tone. A stranger to him once again, she insisted, "It has to be."

Chapter Fourteen

Jeb walked into his parents' ranch house, saw his three siblings, their spouses and his parents, and was tempted to walk right back out.

"What is this, an intervention?" he demanded gruffly, only half kidding. He had answered a summons to talk to his mom, not the whole tribe.

"How'd you guess?" Cutting off his exit, his mother took him by the elbow and guided him into the living room.

Jeb tried to be polite. "I know you-all mean well, but—"

"We're talking to you," his dad said, "whether you like it or not, so you may as well settle in for the long haul."

Jeb could argue with one or two McCabes. But seven at once?

Grimacing, he sat down in the club chair they had apparently reserved for him. He exhaled dramatically. "Get it over with then."

Emily spoke up first. "We want to know why you broke Cady Keilor's heart."

Jeb stared at his little sister. She had gotten far too romantic since her own marriage. But this was ridiculous!

"I what?" It was more like the other way around! Cady had been the one who had been so blunt it hurt. Making love to him as if she meant it, only to tell him later she hadn't!

"I heard you asked Cady to marry you, out of pity," Hank remarked with a disapproving frown.

Holden, always the most serious, added in censure, "Not good, big brother. Not good at all. No woman wants to think of herself as a charity case!"

Jeb harrumphed. "First of all, I did not ask Cady out of pity."

"But you did feel sorry for her?" Shane ascertained with the gruff honesty Jeb had come to expect from his dad.

Seeing no use in sugarcoating what had turned out to be an unmitigated disaster all around, Jeb shrugged. "Who wouldn't have felt sorry for Cady? To go through the entire adoption process for four long years, and finally get selected to be an adoptive parent, only to find out she was rejected—again—at the end? She was heartbroken. As anyone would have been in her place." *And so was I.*

"And you care about her," Greta guessed.

His mother's gentle look had Jeb huffing cantankerously before he could stop himself, "For all the good it's done me. Cady put me in the friend category years ago, and I've never really left it."

Emily blinked. "She acted like you were a heck of a lot more than friends when I saw her talking to Avalynne at my café last week."

"That's because we…" Jeb stopped himself.

"Let things get a little romantic for a change?" She smiled impishly, helping him out.

Jeb nodded gratefully at his baby sister. "That's right," he answered prosaically. "And for the record…" he paused to look everyone in the family in the eye "…my marriage proposal to her was entirely serious." Cady had been the one with cold feet.

Silence fell. No one seemed to be able to understand why she didn't want to take their relationship to the next level, any more than he had. Cady had certainly acted as if she was crazy about him. She had seemed to want him in her life. First as her longtime friend and baby Zoe's godfather, and then a whole lot more.

"Maybe she would have taken you more seriously if the whole thing with Avalynne hadn't happened," Holden theorized.

Hank nodded. "Once you change your mind at the last minute and leave a woman at the altar… Face it, no woman wants to think about the same thing happening to her, down the road. So if Cady shied away for that reason…" His brother shrugged.

Jeb's anger built. "It wasn't that."

"Of course it was," Greta said.

He glared at his mother and enunciated clearly, "No. It wasn't."

"How do you know?" Shane challenged.

"Because—" Jeb gave his father the same censuring look and blurted gruffly "—I told Cady the truth about what really happened that day. She knows—" Abruptly, he realized he had once again said too much.

Everyone in his family leaned forward eagerly. "Knows what?" Holden asked cautiously.

Suddenly, the burden Jeb had been carrying for the last ten years was too much to bear.

"That it wasn't me who called off the wedding that day," Jeb confessed wearily. "It was Avalynne."

Everyone stared at him. In the silence he could have heard a pin drop.

Jeb figured he had revealed this much, so might as well continue. He sighed. "She asked me to take the blame, and I did."

More shock reverberated throughout the room.

"It seemed like the gallant thing to do at the time," he explained.

Emily gaped at him. "But her parents sued you!"

Jeb nodded. He explained how upset his ex had been about that, concluding, "Avalynne has been quietly paying me back, a little at a time, ever since—and Cady knows that, too."

"Maybe so, but…she can't be happy about it," Shane ventured.

Why the hell not? Jeb wondered. "I would think that would raise her estimation of me, not lower it!" Especially since it made him less of a chump.

"Unless," Greta theorized quietly, "Cady interprets those actions to mean you are still tied to Avalynne emotionally."

Jeb rolled his eyes. "That's definitely not true."

"Then maybe she thinks you're the kind of man who goes along to get along, and hence is lacking in character," Shane said.

Jeb glared at his father. "It's taken a lot of strength for me to endure the gossip all these years," he countered.

His parents nodded. "And it would take a lot more for you to set the record straight—with everyone."

There they went again. "I promised Avalynne I would never tell anyone what really happened that day," Jeb confided glumly. "And now I've broken my promise twice."

Oddly enough, no one in his family thought less of him for the breach of promise.

Hank clapped a hand on his shoulder. "Some vows shouldn't be made."

Holden added his brotherly support, "If Avalynne is really your friend, she will understand why you have to set the record straight and clear your name, and finally put an end to that chapter of your life."

Emily nodded soberly, advising, "Because Cady will never take you seriously until you do."

"Vacations—even little ones—are supposed to make people happy," Suki observed from the padded table next to Cady.

Cady cast a glance at her confident older sister. "It's not that. I'm grateful for the day at the spa..." which was Suki and Hermann's post-trip gift to her "...and the gamut of skin, hair and body treatments."

"Good, because when we're done, we are both going to look incredibly beautiful."

For the first time in her life, Cady felt as beautiful as her older sister...and it was all because of Jeb. The way he had made her feel when he looked at her and made love to her, had been an incredible boost to her self-esteem.

She grimaced, her skin resisting the tightness of the customized facial mask. "I'm upset because my friendship with Jeb is over."

Suki removed the cooling gel disks from her eyes. "He didn't mean to hurt you with his proposal."

"I know that, Suki. I know Jeb thinks he was doing

the right thing in asking me to marry him and have his baby." She wrung her hands together. "But I also know that one of these days he's going to realize we are just friends who shared a common goal of surviving the babysitting gig with the boys. Had we not been thrown together that way..." And happened to make hot, wild, love during the process...

Cady shrugged, her throat so congested she couldn't go on. Finally she managed to say, "We were playing house." The grown-up version.

Suki touched her arm, correcting gently, "You were getting a taste of what it is to have a family. And you both liked it. A lot. So did the boys."

The lump in Cady's throat grew. It was all she could do to hold back the tears. "The point is I know he feels sorry for me now because of my loss, and he wants to help because he is so generous of heart."

Suki did not disagree. "I don't know if you realize it, honey, but you sound like a woman in love."

Exactly the point, Cady thought miserably. Unable to sit still a moment longer, she got up and began to pace, full body mask and all. "I adore him. I have for years. You know that.... If I thought it would work long term, I would marry him in an instant. But I can't do that, because one of these days Jeb is going to wake up."

Suki sat up, too. She swung her legs over the edge of the table. "Like he's done with everything else he tried that ultimately didn't feel right?"

Cady nodded, even more dejectedly. "He's going to eventually realize he needs the kind of love that you and Hermann have. And he'll want to be free to pursue other avenues, but will be too noble to hurt me or any kids we might have by that point." She sighed. "The last thing I want is for him to feel trapped and bitter."

Suki lifted a perfectly contoured eyebrow. "So you're saving Jeb McCabe from himself, is that it?"

"Yes."

"What a load of parsnips."

"Excuse me?" she retorted.

Suki leaped off the table and marched over to her. "If anyone is protecting themselves from potential hurt, it's you. I don't know why, because you are so beautiful and smart and talented…."

Cady scowled right back and complained bitterly, "Maybe it's because I always seem to lose out in the end, at least in my personal life."

"So what?" Suki threw up her hands in frustration. "So you've had some losses! Does that mean you have to stop trying to get what you want out of life, which in this case is clearly a life with Jeb McCabe?"

The tears Cady had been fighting flooded her eyes.

Suki wrapped a sisterly arm about her. "Sweetie, I know you've been hurt and disappointed in the past, and I'm sorry about that."

Cady nodded glumly.

"But if you want the kind of romantic, passionate, enduring love that provides a foundation for a lifelong marriage, you are going to have to go out there and risk your tender vulnerable heart to get it."

Suki gave Cady's shoulders an encouraging squeeze and continued even more softly, "Because until you let your guard down, Cady, until you allow yourself to let Jeb all the way past your defenses and excuses, you will never have the love you so richly deserve."

LATE FRIDAY AFTERNOON, Cady's assistant carried the life-size hardboard poster of the Hanover Horseshoes spokesmodel into Cady's office. The two of them stood there for a moment looking at it. Finally, Marissa grinned and said, "Well, the cowboy's cute. No doubt about it." She sighed dreamily and placed a fluttering hand over her heart. "But he doesn't compare with Jeb McCabe."

"You must have paid her to say that," a hauntingly familiar voice teased from the open doorway behind them.

A shiver of awareness danced down her spine as Cady turned and saw Jeb. He wasn't in his usual ranch garb, but a sport coat, shirt and tie that made the most of his broad shoulders and powerful arms and chest. His slacks were creased, his boots polished to a sheen. He had a welcoming smile on his lips and a serious glint in his blue-gray eyes. Cady's heart rose and dipped, then rose again.

This was exactly where the trouble had started three weeks ago.

Yet there was no denying she was glad to see Jeb. The last week of silence had been excruciating.

Marissa caught the emotional sparks arcing between them. She picked up the life-size cardboard cutout once again. "I think I'll just take this outside and give you two your privacy." She exited, shutting the door behind her.

Cady had been practicing for days what she was going to say when the moment came. The only trouble was, now that Jeb was actually here, she didn't know where to begin.

She only knew she didn't want to speak rashly and mess things up between them again.

Jeb studied her expression. "Is this a good time?"

Anytime she was with him was a good time. She could only hope he felt the same way. Cady cleared her throat. "Perfect." She had been about to leave for the day. The Houston traffic could wait.

His eyes never leaving her face, Jeb stepped close enough to take her hands in his. "I wanted to apologize for proposing to you the way I did."

Cady swallowed as the warmth and tenderness of his grip engulfed her. Did that mean he also wanted to take everything else back, as well? The lovemaking, the confidences, the teamwork…not to mention the happiness she had felt when they were together?

Suddenly, she wasn't so sure she wanted to hear what he had to say, if he was going to tell her he wanted to go back to being casual friends, and break her heart all over again. She drew a deep, bolstering breath. "It's not really necessary."

His lips formed a sober downward curve. "Yes, Cady, it is." He tightened his fingers tenderly on hers. "I was out of line. And I was especially wrong for thinking that I could move on with you, without ever really dealing with my past."

Her heart sank yet again. "You're talking about Avalynne."

He nodded, released her and stepped back.

Jeb threaded a hand through his hair. His anguished tone reflected a combination of guilt and regret. "Avalynne wasn't the only one who benefited from the lies about what happened that day. The bad reputation I garnered kept the seriously marriageable women away."

It certainly had, Cady thought.

He swallowed. "As much as it shames me to admit it, I realize—in retrospect—that I liked it that way. My bad rep kept me from having to risk my heart, and served as a handy excuse for why I would never commit long term to anyone or anything again. Because—as legend went—I just wasn't up to the challenge for that kind of commitment...in anything."

His gaze drifted over her lazily as he stepped closer once again. He cupped her shoulders with his palms, and in that instant, all communication between them transformed into something deeper. He inhaled and looked deep into her eyes, admitting, "I would probably still think that way if it hadn't been for you, and your insistence that I start confronting the real problems in my life, and stop living a lie."

The unexpectedness of his admission mingled with her hope for a real future together. "You're going to clear your name?"

"I already have," Jeb told her in satisfaction. "I talked to my family first, and then Avalynne. When she refused to take action with me, I went to see her parents on my own and told them everything."

Shock held Cady motionless. This *was* a big step in the right direction. "How did that go?" she finally managed to ask.

Jeb conceded with a grimace, "Well, at first it was a little ugly. But when Mr. and Mrs. Stone finally understood everything that had happened and why, they said they felt relieved. They were sorry for suing me, and angry with Avalynne for still not coming forward, but they know their daughter has always preferred to run away rather than stay and deal with any problems."

Cady's pulse picked up as she moved restlessly to the window. "So now what?"

Casually, Jeb moved to stand opposite her. "Well, I think it's safe to say that between her parents and mine, everyone in Laramie County is now up to speed on what really happened. Including Suki and Hermann, whom I told in person last night."

Cady's jaw dropped in astonishment. "You did?"

Jeb nodded, his expression serious, intent. "I wanted them to hear it from me."

"They didn't say anything to me," Cady said in confusion.

He braced a shoulder against the glass. "I asked them not to. I told them I was going to see you today, and I wanted to speak to you in person, too, since you are responsible for me moving forward."

Was that all this was? A chance to say thank-you? Cady wondered in disappointment.

She forced herself to be gracious. "Well, I'm glad things have worked out for you." *And sorry they are apparently not going to work out for us, not the way I foolishly hoped, anyway.*

Still, this was her chance to correct her mistakes, too.

She drew a breath and turned away from the rush hour traffic visible on the freeway below. "I'm glad you came to see me today. I wasn't sure you'd ever want to speak to me again, after the harsh way I turned down your proposal."

Jeb's glance narrowed. "You were right to do so," he said, catching her hand before she could slip away. "Ending old gossip by giving people something new to talk about, and hooking up just to have a baby, are both very poor reasons for saying 'I do.'"

Cady thought about how close they had been, during the last couple of weeks, and couldn't resist arguing her point. "It was a little more than that," she found herself saying defensively. "You were there when I needed you, Jeb."

Unable to help herself, she came closer, too, and took his other hand in hers. With both hope and fear welling in her heart, she gazed at him, knowing it was now or never. "You made me realize that I want what I've never really hoped I could have. A deep romantic love, a marriage that will last forever. And," Cady continued in a low trembling voice, "I want to have babies the old-fashioned way, by making love with the man I adore."

Understanding lit his eyes. "Then why haven't you gone after that?" he inquired softly.

Tightening her fingers on his, Cady looked deep into Jeb's eyes and forced herself to be even more forthright. "Because I was afraid to risk my heart, too," she whispered emotionally.

She shrugged and held his penetrating gaze. "I didn't think I would ever be lucky enough to get what I wanted in my personal life the way I had at work, so I figured, instead of being disappointed, I would just settle for less, too. And I think I knew all along—even when I was far too stubborn to admit it to myself—that there was only one man in this world who could give me all those things."

Here was her chance. The moment she had to take that giant leap of faith...

"And that man," Cady continued, with every ounce of feeling and courage in her heart, "is you."

JEB HAD COME TO HOUSTON, hoping to be lucky enough to get a second chance with Cady. Now all his dreams were coming true, too.

She stood on tiptoe and draped her arms about his neck, happiness and hope glittering in her eyes. "I love you, Jeb," she whispered softly.

He wrapped his arms around her and pulled her close, burying his face in the fragrant softness of her hair. "I love you, too, Cady, more than I ever thought was possible."

Their breaths soughed out in relief. Their glances met. Jeb lowered his head and delivered a resounding kiss that left no doubt about the depth of his feelings for her. Finally, he drew back. "For the record," he teased, between soft, sweet kisses, "You've just blown the rest of my big speech to smithereens."

Happiness sparkled in Cady's amber eyes. She cuddled close to him. "You can give me the gist of it."

Jeb kissed the back of her hand and gazed down at her, knowing he had found love at long last. "I came here to ask your permission to court you," he confessed. "The old-fashioned way, the way you deserve."

She wrinkled her pretty nose at the notion, her natural impatience coming to the fore once again. "You don't have to do that, Jeb. We've been friends a long time. I wouldn't mind going from zero to sixty again."

"I wouldn't mind that, either," he admitted, kissing her temple, the sensitive place behind her ear, the smooth slope of her collarbone.

He sat on the edge of her desk and pulled her onto his lap, threading one hand through her hair and wrapping the other about her waist. "But we're also going to do some serious courting, and make sure that you have the engagement—and the wedding—of your dreams." He sealed the vow with another long, leisurely kiss. "And the babies you have always wanted, after that."

anonymous.........the weariness of your that and the
mailed lips of low left his side, her fingers; however busy, would
but less you look before we make our step. Now Buy

Epilogue

"Aunt Cady, how are we going to see what the babies look like if they don't open their eyes?" Dalton asked in frustration.

"And how come there had to be two of them?" Finn added.

"Two girls," Micah added emphatically, as if it were the worst thing on earth.

"Yeah, why couldn't they have been boys?" Dalton pouted.

"I don't get why their names have to be Lily and Rose," Finn harrumphed. "Everybody knows those are flowers."

Cady and Jeb grinned at their three nephews, who had come to the hospital to meet the newest members of the family.

Smiling fondly, Cady handed the twins to their daddy and held out her arms. All three boys climbed up on her hospital bed and settled in the curve of her embrace.

With great reverence, Cady addressed all their concerns. "The babies' eyes are closed because they are sleeping. When the twins wake up, they'll open their eyes. I think the reason we were blessed with girls is that we *already have* three adorable little boys in our family."

The brothers beamed in delight.

"And girls are allowed to be named after flowers," Cady explained.

The two older boys snuggled next to her, listening intently, still a little unsure. Micah hung on tight to Cady, and cuddled on her lap.

"I think I know what the problem is, though," Jeb said, handing off the twins to Suki and Hermann.

His expression as serious as the situation warranted, he sat on the bed next to Cady and the boys. "I think you fellas might be worried that Aunt Cady and I won't have time for you now that we have the babies."

The looks on their faces said Jeb had diagnosed the problem accurately.

"But that's absolutely not true," Cady exclaimed, agreeing with her husband and looking each child in the eye. "Uncle Jeb and I will always have plenty of time for you all. You can come to our ranch and see us whenever you want, and we'll come to your house, too. In fact, your mommy and daddy and Jeb and I have already talked about trading babysitting duties from time to time, so you boys will be able to get Uncle Jeb and I all to yourselves."

"Promise?" Dalton asked, his voice sounding a little rusty.

Cady and Jeb nodded, and said in unison, "We absolutely promise that we will always be here for you."

Delighted, the boys relaxed, and soon were telling Cady and Jeb about their latest exploits in great detail. Finally it was time for them to go.

They said goodbye and left with their mom and dad.

Jeb and Cady were alone with the twins.

With Rose cradled in her arms, she looked over at Jeb. He was so big and strong and handsome, so unbearably tender and loving. Their two daughters would never want for understanding or support. Pure bliss overwhelmed her. "I am so happy."

He nodded, suddenly a little misty, too. "I feel so blessed," he murmured, holding Lily as if she were the greatest gift on earth.

He leaned forward and gently kissed Cady's temple. "And not just because you married me and gave me the children I always wanted." She grinned, and he winked as they both reflected on the fun they'd had doing just that. "But because," Jeb continued huskily, "I finally understand what true happiness and contentment are."

So did Cady.

Six months into their dating life, she had quit her job in Houston, to take one in the marketing department of the Laramie County chamber of commerce.

The job was perfect. She loved devising plans for the local businesses, to boost their bottom line. She could do as much of her work at home as she wanted.

And Jeb was happy professionally, too. He liked his expanded cattle breeding operation so much he had purchased two black baldie bulls and was leasing them out to other ranchers for extra cash.

Financially, they were all set.

But it was the home front where true joy existed.

"Whoever would have thought we could go from being good friends to head over heels in love?" she whispered, amazed at the changes the last two years had brought.

"You and I are proof couples do live happily ever after," Jeb agreed.

And together, they set out to do just that.

* * * * *

Watch for the last story in the
TEXAS LEGACIES: THE MCCABES
miniseries,
A COWBOY TO MARRY,
coming soon only from
Harlequin American Romance.

Harlequin®

COMING NEXT MONTH

Available August 9, 2011

#1365 LAST CHANCE COWBOY
American Romance's Men of the West
Cathy McDavid

#1366 MY TRUE COWBOY
Men of Red River
Shelley Galloway

#1367 RANGER DADDY
Fatherhood
Rebecca Winters

#1368 A MOTHER'S HOMECOMING
Tanya Michaels

You can find more information on upcoming
Harlequin® titles, free excerpts and more at
www.HarlequinInsideRomance.com.

REQUEST YOUR FREE BOOKS!
2 FREE NOVELS PLUS 2 FREE GIFTS!

 Harlequin®

 *American ★ Romance*®

LOVE, HOME & HAPPINESS

YES! Please send me 2 FREE Harlequin® American Romance® novels and my 2 FREE gifts (gifts are worth about $10). After receiving them, if I don't wish to receive any more books, I can return the shipping statement marked "cancel." If I don't cancel, I will receive 4 brand-new novels every month and be billed just $4.49 per book in the U.S. or $5.24 per book in Canada. That's a saving of at least 14% off the cover price! It's quite a bargain! Shipping and handling is just 50¢ per book in the U.S. and 75¢ per book in Canada.* I understand that accepting the 2 free books and gifts places me under no obligation to buy anything. I can always return a shipment and cancel at any time. Even if I never buy another book, the two free books and gifts are mine to keep forever.

154/354 HDN FEP2

Name _____ (PLEASE PRINT)

Address _____ Apt. #

City _____ State/Prov. _____ Zip/Postal Code

Signature (if under 18, a parent or guardian must sign)

Mail to the **Reader Service:**
IN U.S.A.: P.O. Box 1867, Buffalo, NY 14240-1867
IN CANADA: P.O. Box 609, Fort Erie, Ontario L2A 5X3

Not valid for current subscribers to Harlequin American Romance books.

Want to try two free books from another line?
Call 1-800-873-8635 or visit www.ReaderService.com.

* Terms and prices subject to change without notice. Prices do not include applicable taxes. Sales tax applicable in N.Y. Canadian residents will be charged applicable taxes. Offer not valid in Quebec. This offer is limited to one order per household. All orders subject to credit approval. Credit or debit balances in a customer's account(s) may be offset by any other outstanding balance owed by or to the customer. Please allow 4 to 6 weeks for delivery. Offer available while quantities last.

Your Privacy—The Reader Service is committed to protecting your privacy. Our Privacy Policy is available online at www.ReaderService.com or upon request from the Reader Service.

We make a portion of our mailing list available to reputable third parties that offer products we believe may interest you. If you prefer that we not exchange your name with third parties, or if you wish to clarify or modify your communication preferences, please visit us at www.ReaderService.com/consumerschoice or write to us at Reader Service Preference Service, P.O. Box 9062, Buffalo, NY 14269. Include your complete name and address.

HARI1B

*Once bitten, twice shy. That's Gabby Wade's motto—
especially when it comes to Adamson men.
And the moment she meets Jon Adamson her theory
is confirmed. But with each encounter a little something
sparks between them, making her wonder if she's been
too hasty to dismiss this one!*

*Enjoy this sneak peek from ONE GOOD REASON
by Sarah Mayberry, available August 2011
from Harlequin® Superromance®.*

Gabby Wade's heartbeat thumped in her ears as she marched to her office. She wanted to pretend it was because of her brisk pace returning from the file room, but she wasn't that good a liar.

Her heart was beating like a tom-tom because Jon Adamson had touched her. In a very male, very possessive way. She could still feel the heat of his big hand burning through the seat of her khakis as he'd steadied her on the ladder.

It had taken every ounce of self-control to tell him to unhand her. What she'd really wanted was to grab him by his shirt and, well, explore all those urges his touch had instantly brought to life.

While she might not like him, she was wise enough to understand that it wasn't always about liking the other person. Sometimes it was about pure animal attraction.

Refusing to think about it, she turned to work. When she'd typed in the wrong figures three times, Gabby admitted she was too tired and too distracted. Time to call it a day.

As she was leaving, she spied Jon at his workbench in the shop. His head was propped on his hand as he studied blueprints. It wasn't until she got closer that she saw his eyes were shut.

He looked oddly boyish. There was something innocent and unguarded in his expression. She felt a weakening in her resistance to him.

"Jon." She put her hand on his shoulder, intending to shake him awake. Instead, it rested there like a caress.

His eyes snapped open.

"You were asleep."

"No, I was, uh, visualizing something on this design." He gestured to the blueprint in front of him then rubbed his eyes.

That gesture dealt a bigger blow to her resistance. She realized it wasn't only animal attraction pulling them together. She took a step backward as if to get away from the knowledge.

She cleared her throat. "I'm heading off now."

He gave her a smile, and she could see his exhaustion.

"Yeah, I should, too." He stood and stretched. The hem of his T-shirt rose as he arched his back and she caught a flash of hard male belly. She looked away, but it was too late. Her mind had committed the image to permanent memory.

And suddenly she knew, for good or bad, she'd never look at Jon the same way again.

Find out what happens next in ONE GOOD REASON, available August 2011 from Harlequin® Superromance®!

Celebrating

Blaze **10** *years of* red-hot reads

Featuring a special August author lineup of
six fan-favorite authors who have written
for Blaze™ from the beginning!

The Original Sexy Six:

Vicki Lewis Thompson
Tori Carrington
Kimberly Raye
Debbi Rawlins
Julie Leto
Jo Leigh

Pick up all six Blaze™
Special Collectors' Edition titles!

August 2011

Plus visit
HarlequinInsideRomance.com
and click on the Series Excitement Tab
for exclusive Blaze™ 10th Anniversary content!

www.Harlequin.com

HBCELEBRATE0811